"There isn't anything we can do about it? Anything at all?" Lynne was asking.

"No. There isn't anything anybody can do. The lab in Mallorysport has given up trying — except to write a scientifically accurate epitaph for the Fuzzy race."

"But . . . but there must be some way to reverse the process?"

"It's irreversible," Ruth told her. "No matter what we do, nine out of every ten Fuzzies born will be defective, stillborn, or dead within hours. The Fuzzies just can't adapt to the change fast enough. We've seen it on every planet we've ever studied; hundreds of cases on Terra alone. The Fuzzies are in a genetic trap they can't get out of . . . and we can't help them."

FUZZY SAPIENS

(Originally published as
THE OTHER HUMAN RACE)

by

H. Beam Piper

ACE SCIENCE FICTION BOOKS
NEW YORK

FUZZY SAPIENS

An Ace Science Fiction Book

PRINTING HISTORY
Ace edition / 1964
Eighth printing / August 1984

ISBN: 0-441-26195-7

Ace Science Fiction Books are published by The Berkley Publishing Group,
200 Madison Avenue, New York, New York 10016.
PRINTED IN THE UNITED STATES OF AMERICA

I

Victor Grego finished the chilled fruit juice and pushed the glass aside, then lit a cigarette and poured hot coffee into the half-filled cup that had been cooling. This was going to be another Nifflheim of a day, and the night's sleep had barely rested him from the last one and the ones before that. He sipped the coffee, and began to feel himself rejoining the human race.

Staff conferences, all day, of course, with everybody bickering and recriminating. He hoped, not too optimistically, that this would be the end of it. By this evening all the division chiefs ought to know what had to be done. If only they wouldn't come running back to him for decisions they ought to make themselves, or bother him with a lot of nit-picking details. Great God, wasn't a staff supposed to handle staff work?

The trouble was that for the last fifteen years, twelve at least, all the decisions had been made in advance, and the staff work had all been routine, but that had been when Zarathustra had been a Class-III planet and the company had owned it outright. In the Chartered Zarathustra Company, emergencies had simply not been permitted to arise. Not, that was, until old Jack Hollo-

1

way had met a small person whom he had named Little
Fuzzy.

Then everybody had lost their heads. He'd lost his
own a few times, and done some things he now wished
he hadn't done. Most of his subordinates hadn't recovered theirs, yet, and the Charterless Zarathustra Company was operating, if that were the word for it, in a
state of total and permanent emergency.

The cup was half empty, again; he filled it to the top
and lit a fresh cigarette from the old one before crushing
it out. Might as well get it started. He reached to the
switch and flicked on the communication screen across
the breakfast table.

In a moment, Myra Fallada appeared in it. She had
elaborately curled white hair, faintly yellowish, a round
face, protuberant blue eyes, and a lower lip of the sort
associated with the ancient Hapsburg family. She had
been his secretary ever since he had come to Zarathustra,
and she thought that what had happened a week ago in
Judge Pendarvis' court had been the end of the world.

"Good morning, Mr. Grego." She was eyeing his dressing gown and counting the cigarette butts in the ashtray, trying to estimate how soon he'd be down at
his desk. "An awful lot of business has come in this
morning."

"Good morning, Myra. What kind of business?"

"Well, things are getting much worse in the cattle
country. The veldbeest herders are all quitting their
jobs; just flying off and leaving the herds . . ."

"Are they flying off in company aircars? If they are,
have Harry Steefer put out wants for them on stolen-
vehicle charges."

"And the *City of Malverton;* she's spacing out from
Darius today." She went on to tell him about that.

2

"I know. That was all decided yesterday. Just tell them to carry on with it. Now, is there anything I really have to attend to personally? If there is, bundle it up and send it to the staff conference room; I'll handle it there with the people concerned. Rubber-stamp the rest and send it back where it belongs, which is not on my desk. I won't be in; I'm going straight to the conference room. That will be in half an hour. Tell the houseboy he can come in to clean up then, and tell the chef I won't be eating here at all. I'll have lunch off a tray somewhere, and dinner with Mr. Coombes in the Executive Room."

Then he waited, mentally counting to a hundred. As he had expected, before he reached fifty Myra was getting into a flutter.

"Mr. Grego, I almost forgot!" She usually did. "Mr. Evins wants inside the gem-reserve vault; he's down there now."

"Yes, I told him to make inventory and appraisal today. I'd forgotten about that myself. Well, we can't keep him waiting. I'll go down directly."

He blanked the screen, gulped what was left of the coffee and rose, leaving the kitchenette-breakfast room and crossing the short hall to his bedroom, taking off his dressing gown as he went. That he should not have forgotten: the problem represented by the contents of the gem-reserve vault was of greater importance, though of less immediacy, than what was going on in the cattle country.

Up to a week ago, when Chief Justice Pendarvis had smashed the company's charter with a few taps of his gavel, sunstones had been a company monopoly. It had been illegal for anybody but the company to buy sunstones, or for anybody to sell one except to a company

3

gem buyer, but that had been company law, and the Pendarvis decisions had wiped out the company's law-making powers. Sunstone deposits were always too scattered for profitable large-scale mining. They were found by free-lance prospectors, who sold them to the company at the company's prices. Jack Holloway, who had started the whole trouble, had been one of the most successful of prospectors.

Now sunstones were in the open competitive market on Zarathustra, and something would have to be done about establishing a new gem-buying policy. Before he could do that, he wanted to know just how many of them the company had in reserve.

So he had to go down and open the vault, before Conrad Evins, the chief gem buyer, could get in to find out. He knew the combination. So—in case anything happened to him—did Leslie Coombes, the head of the legal division, and, against the possibility that both he and Coombes were killed or incapacitated, there was a copy of it neatly typed on a slip of paper in a special-security box at the Bank of Mallorysport, which could only be gotten out by the Colonial Marshal with a court order. It was a bother, but too many people couldn't be trusted with that combination.

The gem rooms were on the fifteenth level down; they were surrounded by the company police headquarters, and there was only one way in, through a door barred by a heavy steel portcullis. The guard who controlled this sat in a small cubicle fronted by two inches of armor glass; several other guards, with submachine guns, sat or stood behind a low counter in front of it. Harry Steefer, the chief of company police, was there, and so was Conrad Evins, the gem buyer, a small man with graying hair and a bulging brow and narrow chin. With them were two gray-smocked assistants.

"Sorry to keep you gentlemen waiting," he greeted them. "Ready, Mr. Evins?"

Evins was. Steefer nodded to the men inside the armor-glass cubicle; the portcullis rose silently. They entered a bare hallway, covered by viewscreen pickups at either end and with sleep-gas release nozzles on the ceiling. The door at the other end opened, and in the small anteroom beyond they all showed their identity cards to a guard: Evins and his two assistants, the sergeant and the two guards accompanying them, Grego, even Chief Steefer. The guard spoke into a phone; somebody completely out of sight and reach pressed a button or flipped a switch and the door beyond opened. Grego went through alone, and down a short flight of steps to another door, brightly iridescent with a plating of collapsium, like a spaceship's hull or a nuclear reactor.

There was a keyboard, like the keyboard of a linotype machine. He went to it, punching out the letters of a short sentence, then waited ten seconds. The huge door receded slowly, then slid aside.

"All right, gentlemen," he called out. "The vault's open."

Then he walked through, into a circular room beyond. In the middle of it was a round table, its top covered with black velvet, with a wide circular light-shade above it. The wall was lined by a steel cabinet with many shallow drawers. The Chief, a sergeant with a submachine gun, Evins, and his two assistants followed him in. He lit a cigarette, watching the smoke draw up around the light-shade and vanish out the ventilator above. Evins' two assistants began getting out paraphernalia and putting things on the table; the gem buyer felt the black velvet and nodded. Grego put his hand on it, too. It was warm, almost hot.

One of the assistants brought a drawer from the cabinet and emptied it on the table—several hundred smooth, translucent pebbles. For a moment they looked like so much gravel. Then, slowly, they began to glow, until they were blazing like burning coals.

Some fifty million years ago, when Zarathustra had been almost completely covered by seas, there had been a marine life-form, not unlike a big jellyfish, and for a million or so years the seas had abounded with them, and as they died they had sunk into the ooze and been covered by sand. Ages of pressure had reduced them to hard little beans of stone, and the ooze to gray flint. Most of them were just pebbles, but by some ancient biochemical quirk, a few were intensely thermofluorescent. Worn as gems, they would glow from the body heat of the wearer, as they were glowing now on the electrically heated table top. They were found nowhere in the galaxy but on Zarathustra, and even a modest one was worth a small fortune.

"Just for a quick estimate, in round figures, how much money have we in this room?" he asked Evins.

Evins looked pained. He had the sort of mind which detested expressions like "quick estimate," and "round figures."

"Well, of course, the Terra market quotation, as of six months ago, was eleven hundred and twenty-five sols a carat, but that's just the average price. There are premium-value stones . . ."

He saw one of those, and picked it up; an almost perfect sphere, an inch in diameter, deep blood-red. It lay burning in his palm; it was beautiful. He wished he owned it himself, but none of this belonged to him. It belonged to an abstraction called the Chartered—no, Charterless—Zarathustra Company, which represented thousands of stockholders, including a number of other abstractions called Terra-Baldur-Marduk Spacelines, and Interstellar Explorations, Ltd., and the Banking Cartel. He wondered how Conrad Evins felt, working with these beautiful things, knowing how much each of them was worth, and not owning any of them.

"But I can tell you how little they are worth," Evins was saying, at the end of a lecture on the Terra gem market. "The stones in this vault are worth not one millisol less than one hundred million sols."

That sounded like a lot of money, if you said it quickly and didn't think. The Chartered, even the Charterless, Zarathustra Company was a lot of company, too, and all its operations were fantastically expensive. That wouldn't be six months' gross business for the company. They couldn't let the sunstone business live on its reserve.

"This is new, isn't it?" he asked, laying the red globe of light back on the heated table top.

"Yes, Mr. Grego. We bought that less than two months ago. Shortly before the Trial." He captitalized the word; the day Pendarvis beat the company down with his gavel would be First Day, Year Zero, on Zarathustra from now on. "It was bought," he added, "from Jack Holloway."

II

SNAPPING OFF the shiny new stenomemophone, Jack Holloway relit his pipe and pushed back his chair, looking around what had been the living room of his camp before it had become the office of the Commissioner of Native Affairs for the Class-IV Colonial Planet of Zarathustra. It had been a pleasant room, a place where a man could spread out by himself, or entertain the infrequent visitors who came this far into the wilderness. The hardwood floor was scattered with rugs made from the skins of animals he had shot; the deep armchairs and the couch were covered with smaller pelts. Like the big table at which he worked, he had built them himself. There was a reading screen, a metal-cased library of microbooks; the gunrack reflected soft gleams from polished stocks and barrels. And now look at the damn place!

Two extra viewscreens, another communication screen, a vocowriter, a teleprint machine, all jammed together. An improvised table on trestles at right angles to the one at which he sat, its top littered with plans and blueprints and things; mostly things. And this red-upholstered swivel chair; he hated that worst of all. Forty years ago, he'd left Terra to get the seat of his pants off the seat of a chair like that, and here he was in the evening of life—well, late afternoon, call it around second cocktail time—trapped in one.

It wasn't just this room, either. Through the open door he could hear what was happening outside. The thud of axes, and the howl of chain-saws; he was going to miss all those big featherleaf trees from around the house. The machine-gun banging of power-hammers, the clanking and grunting of bulldozers. A sudden warning cry, followed by a falling crash and a multivoiced burst of blasphemy. He hoped none of the Fuzzies had been close enough to whatever had happened to get hurt.

Something tugged gently at his trouser-leg, and a small voice said, "Yeek?" His hands went to his throat, snapping on the ultrasonic hearing-aid and inserting the earplug. Immediately, he began to hear a number of small sounds that had been previously inaudible, and the voice was saying, "Pappy Jack?"

He looked down at the Zarathustran native whose affairs he had been commissioned to administer. He was an erect biped, two feet tall, with a wide-eyed humanoid face, his body covered with soft golden fur. He wore a green canvas pouch lettered TFMC, and a two-inch silver disc on a chain about his neck, and nothing else. The disc was lettered LITTLE FUZZY, and *Jack Holloway, Cold Creek Valley, Beta Continent*, and the numeral *I*. He was the first Zarathustran aborigine he or any other Terran human had ever seen.

He reached down and stroked his small friend's head.

"Hello, Little Fuzzy. You want to visit with Pappy Jack for a while?"

Little Fuzzy pointed to the open door. Five other Fuzzies were peeping bashfully into the room, making comments among themselves.

"Fuzzee no shu do-bizzo do-mitto zat-hakko," Little Fuzzy informed him. *"Heeva so si do-mitto."*

Some Fuzzies who hadn't been here before had just come; they wanted to stay. At least, that was what he thought Little Fuzzy was saying; it had only been ten days since he had known that Fuzzies could talk at all. He pressed a button to start the audiovisual recorder; it was adjusted to transform their ultrasonic voices to audible frequencies.

"Make talk." He picked his way through his hundred-word Fuzzy vocabulary. "Pappy Jack friend. Not hurt, be good to them. Give good things."

"Josso shoddabag?" Little Fuzzy asked. *"Josso shoppo-diggo? Josso t'heet? Esteefee?"*

"Yes. Give shoulder-bags and chopper-diggers and treats," he said. "Give Extee-Three."

Friendly natives; distribution of presents to. Function of the Commissioner of Native Affairs. Little Fuzzy began a speech. This was Pappy Jack, the greatest and wisest of all the Big Ones, the Hagga, the friend of all the People, the Gashta, only the Big Ones called the Gashta Fuzzies. He would give wonderful things. *Shoddabag,* in which things could be carried, leaving the hands free. He displayed his own. And weapons so hard that they never wore out. He ran to the jumbled pile of bedding under the gunrack and came back with a six-inch leaf-shaped blade on a twelve-inch shaft. And Pappy Jack would give the *Hoksu-Fusso,* the Wonderful Food, *esteefee.*

Rising, he went out to what had been his kitchen before it had been crammed with supplies. There were plenty of chopper-diggers; he'd had a couple of hundred made up before he left Mallorysport. Shoulder-bags were in shorter supply. They were all either Navy black or Marine Corps green, first-aid pouches and tool-kit pouches and belt pouches for submachine gun and auto-rifle magazines, all fitted with shoulder straps. He hung five of them over his arm, then unlocked a cupboard and got out two rectangular tins with blue labels marked EMERGENCY FIELD RATION, EXTRATERRESTRIAL SERVICE TYPE THREE. All Fuzzies were crazy about Extee-Three, which demonstrated that, while sapient beings, they were definitely not human. Only a completely starving human would eat the damn stuff.

When he returned, the five newcomers were squat-ting in a circle inside the door with Little Fuzzy, exam-ining his steel weapon and comparing it with the paddle-shaped hardwood sticks they had made for them-selves. The word *zatku* was being frequently used.

It was an important word to Fuzzies, their name for a big pseudocrustacean Terrans called a land-prawn. Fuz-zies hunted *zatku* avidly, and, until they had tasted Extee-Three, preferred them to any other food. If it hadn't been for the *zatku,* the Fuzzies would have stayed in the unexplored country of northern Beta Continent, and it would have been years before any Terran would have seen one.

Quite a few Terrans, especially Victor Grego, the Zarathustra Company manager-in-chief, were wishing the Fuzzies had stayed permanently undiscovered. Zara-thustra had been listed as a Class-III planet, inhabitable by Terran humans but uninhabited by any native race of sapient beings, and on that misunderstanding the Zarathustra Company had been chartered to colonize and exploit it and had been granted outright ownership of the planet and one of the two moons, Darius. The other moon, Xerxes, had been retained as a Federation

Navy base, which had been fortunate, because suddenly Zarathustra had turned into a Class-IV planet, with a native population.

The members of the native population here present looked up expectantly as he opened one of the tins and cut the gingerbread-colored cake into six equal portions. The five newcomers sniffed at theirs and waited until Little Fuzzy began to eat. Then, after a tentative nibble, they gobbled avidly, with full-mouthed sounds of delight.

From the first, he had suspected that they weren't just cute little animals, but people—sapient beings, like himself and like the eight other sapient races discovered since Terrans had gone out to the stars. When Bennett Rainsford, then a field naturalist for the Institute of Xeno-Sciences, had seen them, he had agreed, and had named the species *Fuzzy fuzzy holloway*. They had both been excited, and very proud of the discovery, and neither of them had thought, until it was brought forcibly to their attention, of the effect on the Zarathustra Company's charter.

Victor Grego had thought of that at once; he had fought desperately, viciously, and with all the resources of the company, to prevent the recognition of the Fuzzies as sapient beings and the invalidation of the company's charter. The battle had ended in court, with Jack Holloway charged with murder for shooting a company gunman and a company executive named Leonard Kellogg similarly charged for kicking to death a Fuzzy named Goldilocks. The two cases, tried as one, had hinged on the question of the sapience of the Fuzzies. On the docket, it had been *People of the Colony of Zarathustra* versus *Holloway and Kellogg*. His lawyer, Gus Brannhard, had insisted on referring to it as *Friends of Little Fuzzy* versus *The Chartered Zarathustra Company*.

Little Fuzzy and his friends had won, and with their sapience recognized, the company's charter was out the airlock, and so was the old Class-III Colonial Government, and Space Commodore Napier, the commandant of Xerxes Base, had been compelled, since Zarathustra was without legal government, to proclaim martial rule and supervise the establishment of a new Class-IV Government. He had appointed Bennett Rainsford Governor.

And just who do you suppose Ben Rainsford appointed as Commissioner of Native Affairs?

Well, somebody had to take it, and who'd started all this Fuzzy business, anyhow?

The five newcomers had finished their Extee-Three, and been given their shoulder-bags and their steel chopper-diggers, and were trying the balance of the latter and beheading imaginary land-prawns with them. He opened the other tin of Extee-Three and divided it. This time, they nibbled slowly, with appreciative comments. Little Fuzzy gathered up the two empty tins and put them in the wastebasket.

"How you come this place?" he asked, when Little Fuzzy had rejoined the circle.

They all began talking at once; with Little Fuzzy's help, he got the general sense of it. They had heard strange noises and had come to the edge of the woods, and seen frightening things. But Fuzzies were people; they investigated, even if they were frightened. Then they had seen other people. *Hagga-gashta*, big people, and *shi-mosh-gashta*, people like us.

Little Fuzzy instantly corrected the speaker. *Hagga-gashta* were just Hagga, Big Ones, and *shi-mosh-gashta* were Fuzzies. Why were the Gashta called Fuzzies? Because Pappy Jack said so, that was why. That seemed to settle it.

"But why come this place? You come from other place, far away. Why come here?"

More argument. Little Fuzzy was explaining what he meant, and the newcomers were answering.

"Tell them here are many-many *zatku*. They come, many lights and darks. Many-many."

Fuzzies could count up to five, the fingers of one hand. The other hand had to be used to count with. They could count in multiples of five to a hand of hands, and after that it was many, and then many-many. Somewhere in the mass of Fuzzy study notes that were piling up was a suggestion to see what Fuzzies could do with an abacus.

So, maybe three months ago and six or eight hundred miles north of here, this gang had heard that the country to the south was teeming with *zatku,* and they had joined the *volkerwanderung*. Little Fuzzy and his family had been in the advance-guard; the big rush was still coming. He tried to find out how they had learned of it. Other Fuzzies had told them: that was as far as he could get.

Anyhow, they had gotten into the pass to the north and come down into Cold Creek Valley, and here they were. They had come to the edge of the woods, seen the activity at the camp, and decided, from the presence of other Fuzzies, that there was nothing to hurt them, and had come in.

"Many things to hurt!" Little Fuzzy contradicted, instantly and vehemently. "Must watch all-time. Not go in front of things that move. Not go under things that go up off ground. Not touch strange things. Ask Big

14

Ones what will hurt. Big Ones try not to hurt Fuzzies, Fuzzies must help."

He continued at length; the newcomers exchanged apprehensive glances and low-voiced comments. Finally, he picked up his chopper-digger and rose.

"*Bizzo*," he said. "*Aki-pokko-so*."

Come; I show you. He got that easily enough. "First, show police place," he advised. "Make marks with fingers; get bright things for necks."

"*Hokay*," Little Fuzzy agreed. "Go *polis*, make *fin-gap'int*, get *idee-disko*."

About the time Terrans had mastered classical native Fuzzy, the Fuzzies would all be talking pigin-Fuzzy. The newcomers made way for Little Fuzzy, and trooped outside after him, like tourists following a guide. He watched them cross the open space in front of the house and turn left toward the bridge over the little stream. Then he went back to his desk and made a screen-call to prod up the tentmaker in Red Hill on the order of shoulder-bags—"Maybe tomorrow, Mr. Holloway; we're doing all we can."—and then made a stenomemo about finding more Extee-Three. Then he went back to doodling and scribbling notes on the table of organization and operation-scheme for the Commission of Native Affairs, on which he seemed to be getting nowhere at a terrific speed.

"Hello, Jack. Another gang joined up?"

He raised his head. The speaker was coming in the door, a stocky, square-faced man in blue. There was a lighter oval on the side of his beret, where something had been removed, and the collar of his tunic showed that his major's single star had quite recently replaced a first lieutenant's double bars. He wore a band on his left arm hand-lettered ZNPF, otherwise his uniform was Colonial Constabulary.

"Hello, George. Come in and rest your feet. You look as though they need it."

Major George Lunt, Commandant, Zarathustra Native Protection Force, agreed wearily and profanely, taking off his beret and his pistol-belt and dropping them on the makeshift table. Then, looking around, he went to a chair and lifted from it four loose-leaf books and a fiberboard carton full of papers, marked OLD ATOM-BOMB BOURBON, and set them on the floor. Then he unzipped his tunic, sat down, and got out his cigarettes.

"Office hut's all up, now," he reported. "They're waiting on a scow-load of flooring for it."

"I was talking on screen about that an hour ago. It'll be here by this evening." By this time tomorrow, all this junk could be moved out, and the place would be home again. "Any men coming out on the afternoon boat?"

"Three. They only got the recruiting office opened yesterday, and there isn't any big rush of recruits. Captain Casagra says he'll lend us fifty Marines and some vehicles, temporarily. How many Fuzzies have we, now, with this new bunch?"

He counted mentally. His own family: Little Fuzzy and Mamma Fuzzy and Baby Fuzzy and Mike and Mitzi and Ko-Ko and Cinderella. George Lunt's Fuzzies. Dr. Crippen and Dillinger and Ned Kelly and Lizzie Borden and Calamity Jane. The nine whom they had found at the camp when they returned from Mallorysport after the trial, and the six who came in day before yesterday, and four yesterday morning, and the two last evening, and now this gang.

"Thirty-eight, counting Baby. That's a lot of Fuzzies," he observed.

"You just think it is," Lunt told him. "The patrols we've had out north of here say they're still coming. This time next week, we'll have a couple of hundred."

And before then, the ones who were here would begin to feel overcrowded, and a lot of nice new *shoppo-diggo* would get bloodied. He said so, adding:

"You have a tactical plan for dealing with a native uprising, Major?"

"I've been worrying about it. You know, we could get rid of a lot of them," Lunt said. "Just mention on telecast that we have more Fuzzies than we know what to do with, and we'd have to start rationing them."

They'd have to do that, anyhow. With all the publicity since the trial, everybody was Fuzzy-crazy. Everybody wanted Fuzzies of their own, and where there's a demand, there are suppliers, legitimate or otherwise. It was a wonder the woods weren't full of people catching Fuzzies to sell now. For all he knew, maybe they were.

And a lot of people shouldn't be allowed to have Fuzzies. Not just sadists and perverts, either. People who'd want Fuzzies because the Joneses had them, and then neglect them. People who would get tired of them after a while and dump them outside town. People who couldn't get it through their moronic heads that Fuzzies were people too. So they'd have to set up some regular system of Fuzzy adoption.

He'd thought, at first, of Ruth Ortheris, Ruth van Riebeek she was, now, for that, but she and her husband were needed too urgently here at the camp on the Fuzzy-study program. There were just too many things about Fuzzies neither he nor anybody else knew, yet, and he'd have to find out what was good for them and what wasn't.

He looked at the clock; 0935; that would be 0635 in Mallorysport. After lunch, which would be mid-morning there, he'd call her and find out how soon she'd be coming out.

III

Ruth van Riebeek—she had resigned both her Navy commission and her maiden name simultaneously five days ago—ought, she told herself, to be happy and excited. She was clear out of Navy Intelligence and its dark corridors of deceit and suspicion, and she and Gerd were married, and any scientific worker in the Federation would give anything to be in her place. A whole new science, the study of a new race of sapient beings; why, it was only the ninth time that had happened in the five centuries since the first Terran star-ship left the Sol System. A tiny spot of light—what they really knew about the Fuzzies—surrounded by a twilight zone of what they thought they knew, mostly erroneous. And beyond that, the dark of ignorance, full of strange surprises, waiting to be conquered. And she was in on the very beginning of it. It was a wonderful opportunity.

But wasn't it just one Nifflheim of a way to spend a honeymoon?

When she and Gerd were married, everything was going to be so wonderful. They would spend a lazy week here in the city, just being happy together and making plans and gathering things for their new home.

Then they would go back to Beta Continent, and Gerd would work the sunstone diggings in partnership with Jack Holloway while she kept house, and they would spend the rest of their lives being happy together in the woods, with their four Fuzzies, Id and Superego and Complex and Syndrome.

The honeymoon, as such, had lasted one night, here at the Hotel Mallory. The next morning, before they were through breakfast, Jack Holloway was screening them. Space Commodore Napier had appointed Ben Rainsford Governor, and Ben had immediately appointed Jack Commissioner of Native Affairs, and now Jack was appointing Gerd to head his study and research bureau, taking it for granted that Gerd would accept. Gerd had, taking it for granted that she would agree, as, after a rebellious moment, she had.

After all, weren't they all responsible for what had happened? The Fuzzies certainly weren't; they hadn't gone to law to be declared sapient. All a Fuzzy wanted was to have fun. And they were responsible to the Fuzzies for what would happen to them hereafter, all of them together, Ben Rainsford and Jack Holloway and she and Gerd, and Pancho Ybarra. And now, Lynne Andrews.

Through the open front of the room, on the balcony, she could hear Lynn's voice, half amused and half exasperated:

"You little devils! Bring that back here! *Do-bizzo. So-josso-aki!*"

A Fuzzy—one of the two males, Superego—dashed inside with a lighted cigarette, the other male, Id, and one of the girls, Syndrome, pursuing. She put in her earplug and turned on her hearing-aid, wishing for the millionth time that Fuzzies had humanly audible voices.

Id was clamoring that it was his turn and trying to take the cigarette away from Superego, who pushed him off with his free hand, took a quick puff, and handed it to Syndrome, who began puffing hastily on it. Id started to grab it, then saw the cigarette she was smoking and ran to climb on her lap, pleading:

"Mummy Woof; josso-aki smokko."

Lynne Andrews, slender and blonde, followed them into the room, the earplug wire of her hearing-aid leading down from under the green bandeau around her head. She carried Complex, squirming in her arms. Complex was complaining that Auntie Lynne wouldn't give her *smokko*.

"That's one Terran word they picked up soon enough," Lynne was commenting.

"Let her have one; it won't hurt her." With scientific caution, she added, "It doesn't seem to hurt them."

She knew what Lynne was thinking. She had been recruited—shanghaied would probably be a better word—from Mallorysport General Hospital because they had wanted somebody whose M.D. was a little less a matter of form than hers or Pancho Ybarra's. Lynne was a pediatrician, which had seemed appropriate because Fuzzies were about the size of year-old human children and because a pediatrician, like a veterinarian, has to be able to get along with a minimum of cooperation from the patient. Unfortunately, she was carrying it beyond analogy and equating Fuzzies with human children. A year-old human oughtn't to be allowed to smoke, so neither should a Fuzzy, who might be fifty for all anybody knew to the contrary.

She gave Id her cigarette. Lynne, apparently much against her better judgment, sat down on a couch and lit one for Complex, and one for herself, and then lit a third for Superego. Now all the Fuzzies had *smokko*. Syndrome ran to one of the low cocktail tables and came back with an ashtray, which she put on the floor. The others sat down with her around it, all but Id, who stayed on Mummy Woof's lap.

"Lynne, they won't take anything that hurts them," she argued. "Alcohol, for instance."

Lynne had to agree. Any Fuzzy would take a drink, just to do what the Big Ones were doing—once. The smallest quantity affected a Fuzzy instantly, and a tipsy Fuzzy was really something to see, and then the Fuzzy would have a sick hangover, and never took a second drink. That was one of the things she'd found out while working with Ernst Mallin, the Company psychologist, and doublecrossing him and the company for Navy Intelligence.

"Well, some of them don't like *smokko*."

"Some human-type people don't, either. Some human-type people have allergies. What kind of allergies do Fuzzies have? That's something else for you to find out."

She set Id on the table and pulled one of the loose-leaf books toward her, picking up a pen and writing the word at the top of the blank page. Id picked up another pen and began making a series of little circles on a notepad.

The door from the hallway opened into the next room; she heard Pancho Ybarra's voice and her husband laughing. The three on the floor put their cigarettes in the ashtray and jumped to their feet, shrieking, "Pappy Ge'hd! Unka Panko!" and dashed through the door into the next room. Id, dropping the pen, jumped down and ran after them. In a moment, they were all back. Syndrome had a Navy officer's cap on her head, holding it up with both hands to see from under it. Id followed, with Gerd's floppy gray sombrero, and Complex and Superego came in carrying a bulky briefcase between them. Gerd and Pancho followed. Gerd's suit, freshly pressed that morning, already rumpled, but the Navy psychologist was still miraculously handbox-neat. She rose and greeted them, kissing Gerd; Pancho crossed to the couch and sat down with Lynne.

"Well, what's new?" Gerd asked.

"Jack called me, about an hour ago. They have the lab hut up, and all the equipment they have for it moved in. They have some bungalows up, a double one for us. Jack showed me a view of it; it's nice. And I was bullying people about the computer and the rest of the stuff. We can all go out as soon as we have everything here together."

"This evening, if we want to run ourselves ragged and get in in the middle of the night," Gerd said. "After lunch tomorrow, if we want to take our time. Ben Rainsford wants us for dinner this evening."

Lynne thought that sounded a trifle cannibalistic, and voted for tomorrow. "How did you make out at the hospital?" she asked.

"They gave us everything we asked for, no argument at all," Gerd said. "And the same at Science Center. I was surprised."

"I wasn't," Pancho said. "There's a lot of scuttlebutt about the Government taking both over. In a couple of weeks, we may be their bosses. What are we going to do about lunch; go out or have it sent in?"

"Let's have it sent in," she said. "We can check over these equipment lists, and you two can chase up anything that's left out this afternoon."

Pancho got out his cigarette case, and discovered that it was empty.

"Hey, Lynne; *so-josso-aki smokko*," he said.

Well, it would be a honeymoon. Sort of crowded, but fun. And Pancho and Lynne were beginning to take an interest in each other. She was glad of that.

Chief Justice Frederic Pendarvis leaned his elbows on the bench and considered the three black-coated lawyers before him in the action of *John Doe, Richard Roe,* et alii, *An Unincorporated Voluntary Association,* versus *The Colonial Government of Zarathustra.*

One, at the defendants' lectern, was a giant; well over six feet and two hundred pounds, his big-nosed face masked by a fluffy gray-brown beard, an unruly mop of gray-brown hair suggesting, incongruously, a halo. His name was Gustavus Adolphus Brannhard, and until he had been rocketed to prominence in what everybody was calling the Fuzzy Trial, he had been chiefly noted for his ability to secure the acquittal of obviously guilty clients, his prowess as a big-game hunter, and his capacity, without visible effect, for whisky. For the past five days, he had been Attorney-General of the Colony of Zarathustra.

The man standing beside and slightly behind him would have seemed tall, too, in the proximity of anybody but Gus Brannhard. He was slender and suavely elegant, and his thin, aristocratic features wore an habitually half-bored, half-amused expression, as though life were a joke he had heard too many times before. His name was Leslie Coombes, he was the Zarathustra Company's chief attorney, and from the position he had taken it looked as though he were here to support his

24

erstwhile antagonist in *People* versus *Holloway and Kellogg*.

The third, at the plaintiff's lectern, was Hugo Ingermann; Judge Pendarvis was making a determined effort not to let that prejudice him against his clients. To his positive knowledge, Ingermann had been in court at least seven times in the last six years representing completely honest and respectable people, and it was possible, though scarcely probable, that this might be the eighth occasion. He was, of course, a member of the Bar, due to lack of evidence to support disbarment proceedings, so he had a right to stand here and be heard.

"This is an action, is it not, to require the Colonial Government to make available for settlement and exploitation lands now in the public domain, and to set up offices where claims to such lands may be filed?" he asked.

"It is, your Honor. I represent the plaintiffs," Ingermann said. He was shorter than either of the others; plump, with a smooth, pink-cheeked face, and beginning to lose his hair in front. There was an expression of complete and utter sincerity in his round blue eyes which might have deceived anybody who had not been on Zarathustra long enough to have heard of him. He would have continued had Pendarvis not turned to Brannhard.

"I represent the Colonial Government, your Honor; we are contesting the plaintiff's action."

"And you, Mr. Coombes?"

"I represent the Charterless Zarathustra Company," Coombes said. "We are not a party to this action. I am here merely as observer and *amicus curiae*."

"The . . . Charterless, did you say, Mr. Coombes? . . . Zarathustra Company has a right to be so represented here; they have a substantial interest." He wondered whose idea "Charterless" was; it sounded like a typical piece of Grego gallows-humor. "Mr. Ingermann?"

"Your Honor, it is the contention of the plaintiffs whom I here represent that since approximately eighty percent of the land surface of this planet is now public domain, by virtue of a recent ruling of the Honorable Supreme Court, it is now obligatory upon the Colonial Government to make this land available to the public. This, your Honor, is plainly stated in Federation Law ..."

He began citing acts, sections, paragraphs; precedents; relevant decisions of Federation Courts on other planets. He was talking entirely for the record; all this had been included in the brief he had submitted. It should be heard, but enough was enough.

"Yes, Mr. Ingermann; the Court is aware of the law, and takes notice that it has been upheld in other cases," he said. "The Government doesn't dispute this, Mr. Brannhard?"

"Not at all, your Honor. Far from it. Governor Rainsford is, himself, most anxious to transfer unseated land to private ownership ..."

"Yes, but when?" Ingermann demanded. "How long is Governor Rainsford going to drag his feet . . ."

"I question the justice of Mr. Ingermann's so characterizing the situation," Brannhard interrupted. "It must be remembered that it is less than a week since there was any public land at all on this planet."

"Or since the Government Mr. Ingermann's clients are suing has existed," Coombes added. "And I could endure knowing who these Messieurs Doe and Roe are. The names sound faintly familiar, but . . ."

"Your Honor, my clients are an association of individuals interested in acquiring land," Ingermann said. "Prospectors, woodsmen, tenant farmers, small veldbeest ranchers . . ."

"Loan-sharks, shylocks, percentage grubstakers, speculators, would-be claim brokers," Brannhard continued.

"They are the common people of this planet!" Ingermann declared. "The workers, the sturdy and honest farmers, the frontiersmen, all of whom the Zarathustra Company has held in peonage until liberated by the great and historic decisions which bear your Honor's name."

"Just a moment," Coombes almost drawled. "Your Honor, the word 'peonage' has a specific meaning at law. I must deny most vehemently that it has ever described the relationship between the Zarathustra Company and anybody on this planet."

"The word was ill-chosen, Mr. Ingermann. It will be deleted from the record."

"We still haven't found out who Mr. Ingermann's clients are, your Honor," Brannhard said. "May I suggest that Mr. Ingermann be placed on the stand and asked to name them?"

Ingermann shot a quick, involuntary glance at the witness stand: a heavy chair, with electrode attachments and a bright metal helmet over it, and a translucent globe on a standard. Then he began clamoring protests. So far, Hugo Ingermann had always managed to avoid having to testify to anything under veridication. That was probably why he was still a member of the Bar, instead of a convict.

"No, Mr. Brannhard," he said, with real sadness. "Mr. Ingermann is not compelled to divulge the names of his clients. Mr. Ingermann would be within his rights in bringing this action on his own responsibility, out of his deep love of justice and well-known zeal for the public welfare."

Brannhard shrugged massively. Nobody could blame him for not trying. Coombes spoke:

"Your Honor, we are all agreed about the Government's obligation, but has it occurred, either to Mr. Ingermann or to the Court, that the present Government is merely a fiat-government set up by military authority? Commodore Napier acted, as he was obliged to, as the ranking officer of the Terran Federation Armed Forces present, to constitute civil government to replace the former one, declared illegal by your Honor. Until elections can be held and a popularly elected Colonial Legislature can be convened, there may be grave doubts as to the validity of some of Governor Rainsford's acts, especially in granting titles to land. Your Honor, do we want to see the courts of this planet vexed, for years to come, with litigation over such titles?"

"That's the Government's attitude precisely," Brannhard agreed. "We're required by law to hold such elections within a year; to do that we'll have to hold an election for delegates to a constitutional convention and get a planetary constitution adopted. That will take six to eight months. Until this can be done, we petition the Court to withhold action on this matter."

"That's quite reasonable, Mr. Brannhard. The Court recognizes the Government's legal obligation, but the Court does not recognize any immediacy in fulfilling it. If, within a year, the Government can open the public lands and establish land-claim offices, the Court will be quite satisfied." He tapped lightly with his gavel. "Next case, if you please," he told the crier.

"Now I see it!" Ingermann almost shouted. "The Zarathustra Company's taken over this new Class-IV

Government, and the courts along with it!"

He hit the bench again with his gavel; this time it cracked like a rifle shot.

"Mr. Ingermann! You are not deliberately placing yourself in contempt, are you?" he asked. "No? I'd hoped not. Next case, please."

Leslie Coombes accepted the cocktail with a word of absent-minded thanks, tasted it, and set it down on the low table. It was cool and quiet up here on the garden-terrace around Victor Grego's penthouse at the top of Company House; the western sky was a conflagration of sunset reds and oranges and yellows.

"No, Victor; Gus Brannhard is not our friend. He's not our enemy, but as Attorney-General he is Ben Rainsford's lawyer, and the Government's—at the moment, it's hard to distinguish between the two—and Ben Rainsford hates all of us vindicatively."

Victor Grego looked up from the drink he was pouring for himself. He had a broad-cheeked, wide-mouthed face. A few threads of gray were visible in the sunset glow among the black at his temples; they hadn't been there before the Fuzzy Trial.

"I don't see why," he said, "It's all over now. They made their point about the Fuzzies; that was all they were interested in, wasn't it?"

He was being quite honest about it, too, Coombes thought. Grego was simply incapable of animosity about something that was over and done with.

"It was all Jack Holloway and Gerd van Riebeek were interested in. Brannhard was their lawyer; he'd have fought just as hard to prove that bush-goblins were sapient beings. But Rainsford is taking this personally. The Fuzzies were his great scientific discovery, and we tried to discredit it, and that makes us Bad Guys. And in the last chapter, the Bad Guys should all be killed or sent to jail."

Grego stoppered the cocktail jug and picked up his glass.

"We haven't come to the last chapter yet," he said. "I don't want any more battles; we haven't patched up the combat damage from the last one. But if Ben Rainsford wants one, I'm not bugging out on it. You know, we could make things damned nasty for him." He sipped slowly and set the glass down. "This so-called Government of his is broke; you know that, don't you? And it'll take from six to eight months to get a Colonial Legislature organized and in session, and he can't levy taxes by executive decree; that's purely a legislative function. In the meantime, he'll have to borrow, and the only place he can borrow is from the bank we control."

That was the trouble with Victor. If anybody or anything challenged him, his first instinct was to hit back. Following that instinct when he had first heard of the Fuzzies had gotten the Company back of the eightball in the first place.

"Well, don't do any fighting with planet busters at twenty paces," he advised. "Gus Brannhard and Alex Napier, between them, talked him out of prosecuting us for what we did before the trial, and convinced him he'd wreck the whole planetary economy if he damaged the company too badly. We're in the same spot; we can't afford to have a bankrupt Government on top of everything else. Let him borrow all the money he wants."

"And then tax it away from us to pay it back?"

"Not if we get control of the Legislature and write the tax laws ourselves. This is a political battle; let's use political weapons."

"You mean organize a Zarathustra Company Party?" Grego laughed. "You have any idea how unpopular the company is, right now?"

"No, no. Let the citizens and voters organize the parties. We'll just pick out the best one and take it over. All we'll need to organize will be a political organization."

Grego smiled slowly over the rim of his glass and swallowed.

"Yes, Leslie. I don't think I need to tell you what to do. You know it better than I do. Have you anybody in mind to head it? They shouldn't be associated with the Company at all; at least, not out where the public can see it."

He named a few names—independent business men, freeholding planters, professional people, a clergyman or so. Grego nodded approvingly at each.

"Hugo Ingermann," he said.

"Good God!" Coombes doubted his ears for a moment. Then he was shocked. "We want nothing whatever to do with that fellow. Why, there isn't a crooked operation in Mallorysport, criminal or just plain dishonest, that he isn't mixed up in. And I told you how he was talking in court today."

Grego nodded again. "Precisely. Well, we won't have anything to do with him. We'll just let Hugo go his malodorous way, and cash in on any scandals he creates. You say Rainsford thinks in terms of Good Guys and Bad Guys? Well, Hugo Ingermann is the baddest Bad Guy on the planet, and if Rainsford doesn't know that, and he probably doesn't, Gus Brannhard'll tell him. I just hope Hugo Ingermann goes on attacking the company every time he opens his mouth." He finished what was in his glass and unstoppered the jug. "Still with me,

Leslie? It's a half hour yet to dinner."

As Gus Brannhard started across the lawn on the south side of Government House, two Fuzzies came dashing to meet him. Their names were Flora and Fauna, and as usual he had to pause and remember that fauns were male and that Flora was a regular feminine name. The names some people gave Fuzzies. Of course, Ben was a naturalist. If he had a pair of Fuzzies of his own, he'd probably have called them Felony and Misdemeanor, or Misfeasance and Malfeasance. He put in his earphone and squatted to get down to their level.

"Hello, sapient beings. Now keep your hands out of Uncle Gus's whiskers." He glanced up and saw the small man with the red beard approaching. "Hello, Ben. They pull yours much?"

"Sometimes. I haven't so much to pull. Yours is more fun. Jack Holloway says they think you're a Big Fuzzy." The Fuzzies were pointing across the lawn, clamoring for him to come and see something. "Oh, sure; their new home. I'll bet there isn't a Fuzzy anywhere has a nicer home. *Hokay*, kids; *bizzo*."

The new home was a Marine Corps pup-tent, pitched in an open glade beside a fountain; it would be a lot roomier for two Fuzzies than for two Marines. There were Fuzzy treasures scattered around it, things from toy shops, and odds and ends of bright or colored or oddly-shaped junk they had scavenged for themselves. He noticed, and commented on, a stout toy wheelbarrow.

"Oh, yes; we have discovered the wheel," Ben said. "They were explaining it to me yesterday; very intelligently, as far as I could follow. They give each other rides, and they are very good about taking turns. And they use it to collect loot. Very good about that, too;

always ask if they can have anything they find."

"Well, this is just wonderful," he told them, and then repeated it in Fuzzy. Ben complimented him on his progress in the language.

"I damn well better learn it. Pendarvis is going to set up a Native Cases Court, like the ones on Loki and Gimli and Thor. Be anybody's guess how soon I'll have to listen to a flock of Fuzzy witnesses."

He looked inside the tent. The blankets and cushions were all piled at one end; bedmaking, it seemed, wasn't a Fuzzy accomplishment. A bed was to sleep in, and no Fuzzy could see the sense in making a bed and then having to un-make it before he could use it. He looked at some of their things, and picked up a little knife, trying the edge on his thumb. Immediately, Flora cried out:

"Keffu, Unka Gus! Sha'ap; kuttsu!"

"Muhgawd, Ben; you hear what she said? She speaks Lingua Terra!"

"That's right. That was one of the first things I taught them. And you don't have to teach them anything more than once, either." He looked at his watch, and spoke to the Fuzzies. They seemed disappointed, but Fauna said, *"Hokay,"* and ran into the tent, bringing out his shoulder-bag and chopper-digger, and Flora's. "Told them we have to make Big One talk, to go hunt land-prawns. I had a bunch brought in, this morning, and turned loose for them."

Fauna piled into the wheelbarrow; Flora got between the shafts and picked it up, starting off at a run, the passenger whooping loudly. Ben watched them vanish among the shrubbery, and got out his pipe and tobacco.

"Gus, why in Nifflheim did Leslie Coombes show up in court today and back you against this fellow Ingermann?" he demanded. "I thought Grego put Ingermann up to that himself."

That's right; any time anything happens, blame Grego.

"No, Ben. The company doesn't want a big land-rush starting, any more than we do. They don't want their whole labor force bugging out on them, and that's what it would come to. I don't know why I can't pound it into your head that Victor Grego has as big a stake in keeping things together on this planet as you have."

"Yes, if he can control it the way he used to. Well, I'm not going to let him . . ."

He made an impatient noise. "And Ingermann; Grego wouldn't touch him with a ten-light-year pole. You call Grego a criminal? Well, maybe you were too busy, over on Beta, counting tree rings and checking on the love life of bush-goblins, to know about the Mallorysport underworld, but as a criminal lawyer I had to. Beside Hugo Ingermann, Victor Grego is a saint, and they have images of him in all the churches and work miracles with them. You name any kind of a racket—dope, pros-titution, gambling, protection-shakedowns, illicit-gem buying, shylocking, stolen goods—and Ingermann's at the back of it. This action of his, today; he has a ring of crooks who want to make a killing in land speculation. That's why I wanted to stop him, and that's why Grego sent Coombes to help me. Ben, you're going to find that this is only the first of many occasions when you and Grego are going to be on the same side."

Rainsford started an angry reply; before he could speak, Gerd van Riebeek's voice floated down from the escalator-head on the terrace above.

"Anybody home down there?"

"No, nobody but us Fuzzies," Rainsford called back.
"Come on down."

IV

WITH A sigh of relief, Victor Grego entered the living room of his penthouse apartment. His hand rose to the switch beside the door, then dropped; the faint indirect glow from around the edge of the ceiling was enough. He'd just pour himself a drink and sit here in the crepuscular silence, resting. His body was tired, more so than it should be, at his age, but his brain was still racing at top speed. No use trying to go to sleep now.

He took off his jacket and neckcloth and dropped them on a chair, opening his shirt collar as he went to the cellaret; he poured a big inhaler-glass half full of brandy and started for his favorite chair, then returned to get the bottle. It would take more than one glass to brake the speeding wheels inside his head. He placed the bottle on a low table, beside the fluted glass bowl, and sat down, wondering what he had noticed that had disturbed him. Nothing important; he sipped from the glass and leaned back, closing his eyes.

They had the trouble in the veldbeest country on Beta and Delta Continents worked out, at least to where they knew what to do about it. Close down all the engineering jobs, the Big Blackwater drainage project on

Beta, and the various construction jobs, and shift men to the cattle ranges; issue them combat equipment and put them on fighting pay, to deal with these gangs of rustlers that were springing up. Maybe if they started a couple of range-wars, Ian Ferguson and his Colonial Constabulary would have to take a hand. But the main thing was to keep the herds together. And the wild veldbeest; Ben Rainsford was a conservationist, he ought to be interested in protecting them.

And he still hadn't decided on a sunstone buying policy. Not enough information on the present situation. He'd have to do something about that.

Oh, Niefflheim with it; think about it tomorrow.

He drank more brandy, and reached to the glass bowl on the low table, and found that it was empty. That was what had bothered him. It had been half full of the sort of tidbits he privately called nibblements—salted nuts, wafers, things like that—when he and Leslie Coombes had gone through the room on their way down for dinner.

Or had it? Maybe he just thought it had been. He began worrying about that, too. And the way he'd forgotten, this morning, about the sunstone inventory. Better call in Ernst Mallin to give him a checkup.

Then he laughed mirthlessly. If anybody needed a checkup, it was the company psychologist himself. Poor Ernst; he'd had a pretty shattering time of it, and now he probably thought he was being blamed for everything.

He wasn't, of course. Mallin had done the best anybody could have done, in an impossible situation. The Fuzzies had been sapient beings, and that was all there'd been to it, and that wasn't Mallin's fault. That Mallin had been forced so to testify in court had been the fault of his immediate subordinate, Dr. Ruth Ortheris, who had also, it developed, been Lieutenant j.g. Ortheris, TFN Intelligence. She'd been the one who tipped Navy Intelligence about the Fuzzies in the first place. She'd been the one who'd smuggled Jack Holloway's Fuzzy family out of Science Center after Leslie Coombes had gotten hold of them on a bogus court order. And she'd been the one who'd insisted on live-trapping that other Fuzzy family and exposing Mallin to them.

That had been a beautiful piece of work. He'd watched the trial by screen; he could still see poor Mallin on the stand, trying to insist that Fuzzies were just silly little animals, with the red-blazing globe of the veridicator calling him a liar every time he opened his mouth. Why, she'd made the company defeat itself with its own witness.

He ought to hate her for that. He didn't; he admired her for it, as he admired anybody who had a job to do and did it competently. He had too damned few people like that in his own organization.

Have to do something nice for Ernst, though. He couldn't stay in charge at Science Center, but he'd have to be promoted out of it. Probably have to invent a job for him.

Finally, he decided that he could go to sleep, now. He took the brandy bottle back to the cellaret, gathered up the garments he had thrown down, and went into the bedroom, putting on the lights.

Then he looked at the bed and saw the golden-furred shape snuggled against the pillows. He swore. One of those life-size Fuzzy dolls that had been on sale ever since the Fuzzies had gotten into the news. If this was somebody's idea of a joke . . .

Then the thing he had taken for a doll sat up, blinked, and said, "Yeek?"

"Why, the damn thing's alive!" he yelled. "It's a *real* Fuzzy!" The Fuzzy was afraid; watching him and at the same time seeking an avenue of escape. "Don't be scared, kid," he soothed. "I won't hurt you. How'd you get in here, anyhow?"

One thing, the puzzle of the empty bowl was solved; the contents were now inside the Fuzzy. This, however, posed the question of how the Fuzzy got there. When he had thought this was a joke, he had been angry. Now he doubted that it was a joke, and he was on the edge of being worried.

The Fuzzy, who had been regarding him warily, had evidently decided that he was not hostile and might even be friendly. He got to his feet, tried to walk on the yielding pneumatic mattress, and tumbled heels-over-head. Instantly he was on his feet again, leaping twice his height into the air, bouncing, and yeeking happily. He caught him on the second bounce and sat down on the bed with him.

"Are you hungry, kid?" That bowl of nibblements wasn't much of a meal, even for a Fuzzy. The stuff was all heavily salted, too. "Bet you're thirsty." What was it Jack Holloway's Fuzzies called him? Pappy Jack. "Well, Pappy Vic'll get you something."

In the kitchenette-breakfast room, the uninvited guest drank two small aperitif-glasses of water and part of a third, while his host wondered about what he'd like to eat. Jack Holloway gave his Fuzzies Extee-Three, but he didn't have . . . Oh, yes; maybe he did.

He went into the bedroom and opened one of the closets, where his field equipment was kept—rifles, sleeping-bag, cameras and binoculars, and a couple of rectangular steel cases to be carried in an aircar, full of camping paraphernalia. He opened one, which contained mess-gear he'd brought with him from Terra and used on field trips ever since, and sure enough, there were a couple of tins of Extee-Three.

The Fuzzy, who had been watching beside him, yeeked exictedly when he saw the blue labels, and ran ahead of him to the kitchenette. He could hardly wait till the tin was open. Somebody had given him Extee-Three before.

He made a sandwich for himself and sat down at the table while the Fuzzy ate, and he was still worried. There were only four doors into Company House from the ground, and all of them were constantly guarded. There were no windows less than sixty feet from the ground. While no bet on what Fuzzies couldn't do was really safe, he doubted that they had learned to pilot aircars just yet. So somebody had brought this Fuzzy here, and beside *How,* which would be by aircar, the question branched out into *When* and *Who* and *Why.*

Why was what worried him most. Fuzzies, as he didn't need to remind himself, were people, and wards of the Terran Federation, and all sort of crimes could be committed against them. Leonard Kellogg would have been executed for killing one of them, if he hadn't done the job for himself in his cell at the jail. And beside murder, there was abduction, and illegal restraint. Maybe somebody was trying to frame him.

He put on the communication screen and punched the call combination of the Chief's office at company police headquarters. He got Captain Morgan Lansky, who held down Chief Steefer's desk from midnight to six. As soon as Lansky saw who was calling, he got rid of his cigar, zipped up his tunic, and tried to look alert, wide awake and busy.

"Why, Mr. Grego! Is anything wrong?"

"That's what I want to know, Captain. I have a Fuzzy up here in my apartment. I want to know how he got here."

"A Fuzzy? Are you sure, Mr. Grego?"

He stooped and picked up his visitor, setting him on the table. The Fuzzy was clutching half a cake of Extee-Three. He saw Lansky looking out of the wall at him and yeeked in astonishment.

"What is your opinion, Captain?"

Captain Lansky's opinion was that he'd be damned. "How did he get in, Mr. Grego?"

Grego prayed silently for patience. "That is precisely what I want to know. To begin with, have you any idea how he got in the building?"

"Somebody," the captain decided, after deliberation, "must have brought him in. In an aircar," he added, after more cogitation.

"I had gotten that far, myself. Would you have any idea when?"

Lansky began to shake his head. Then he was smitten with an idea.

"Hey, Mr. Grego! The pilfering!"

"What pilfering?"

"Why, the pilfering. Pilfering, and ransacking; in offices and like that. And somebody's getting into supply rooms at some of the cafeterias, and where they keep the candy and stuff for the vending robots. The first musta been the night of the sixteenth." That would be three days ago. "The first report came in day before yesterday morning, after the 0600-1200 shift came on. It's been like that ever since; every morning, places being ransacked and candy and stuff like that taken. You think that Fuzzy's been doing all of it?"

He could see no reason why not. Fuzzies were small people, able to make themselves very inconspicuous when they wanted to. Hadn't they survived for oomphty-thousand years in the woods, dodging harpies and bush-goblins. And Company House was full of hiding places. It had been built twelve years ago, three years after he came to Zarathustra, and it had been built big. It wasn't going to be like the buildings they ran up on Terra, to be torn down in a couple of decades; it was meant to be the headquarters of the Chartered Zarathustra Company for a couple of centuries. Eighteen levels, six to eight floors to a level; more than half of them were empty and many unfinished, waiting for the CZC to grow into them.

"The ones Dr. Jimenez trapped for Dr. Mallin," Lansky said. "Maybe this is one of them."

He winced, mentally, at the thought of those Fuzzies. Catching them and letting Mallin study them had been the worst error of the whole business, and the way they had gotten rid of them had been a close runner-up.

It had been a Mallorysport police lieutenant, on his own lame-brained responsibility, who had started the story about a ten-year-old girl, Lolita Lurkin, being attacked by Fuzzies, and it had been Resident-General Nick Emmert, now bound for Terra aboard a destroyer from Xerxes to face malfeasance charges, who had posted a reward of five thousand sols apiece on Jack Holloway's Fuzzies, supposed to be at large in the city. Dead or alive; that had touched off a hysterical Fuzzy-hunt.

That had been when he and Leslie Coombes had perpetrated their own masterpiece of imbecility, by turning loose the Fuzzies Mallin had been studying, whom everybody was now passionately eager to see the last of, in the hope that they would be shot for Emmert's reward money. Instead, Jack Holloway, hunting for his own Fuzzies in ignorance of the fact that they were safe on Xerxes Naval Base, had found them, and now he was very glad of it. Gerd and Ruth van Riebeek had them now.

"No, Captain. Those Fuzzies are all accounted for. And Dr. Jimenez didn't bring any others to Mallorysport."

That put Lansky back where he had started. He went off on another tangent:

"Well, I'll send somebody up right away to get him, Mr. Grego."

"You will do nothing of the sort, Captain. The Fuzzy's quite all right here; I'm taking care of him. All I want to know is how he got into Company House. And I want the investigation made discreetly. Tell the Chief when he comes in." He thought of something else. "Get hold of a case of Extee-Three; do it before you go off duty. And have it put on my delivery lift, where I'll find it the first thing tomorrow."

The Fuzzy was disappointed when he blanked the screen; he wondered where the funny man in the wall had gone. He finished his Extee-Three, and didn't seem to want anything else. Well, no wonder; one of those cakes would keep a man going for twenty-four hours.

He'd have to fix up some place for the Fuzzy to sleep. And some way for him to get water; the sink in the kitchenette was too high to be convenient. There was a low sink outside, which the gardener used; he turned the faucet on slightly, set a bowl under it, and put a little metal cup beside it. The Fuzzy understood about that, and yeeked appreciatively. He'd have to get one of those earphones the Navy people had developed, and learn the Fuzzy language.

Then he remembered that Fuzzies were most meticulous about their sanitary habits. Going back inside, he entered the big room behind the kitchenette which served the chef as a pantry, the houseboy for equipment storage, the gardener as a seedhouse and tool shed, and all of them as a general junkroom. He hadn't been inside the place, himself, for some time. He swore disgustedly when he saw it, then began rummaging for something the Fuzzy could use as a digging tool.

Selecting a stout-handled basting spoon, he took it out into the garden and dug a hole in a flower bed, sticking the spoon in the ground beside it. The Fuzzy knew what the hole was for, and used it, and then filled it in and stuck the spoon back where he found it. He made some ultrasonic remarks, audible as yeeks, in gratification at finding that human-type people had civilized notions about sanitation too.

Find him something better tomorrow, a miniature spade. And fix up a real place for him to sleep, and put in a little fountain, and . . .

It suddenly occurred to him that he was assuming that the Fuzzy would want to stay with him permanently, and also to wonder whether he wanted a Fuzzy living with him. Of course he did. A Fuzzy was fun, and fun was something he ought to have more of. And a Fuzzy would be a friend. A Fuzzy wouldn't care whether he was manager-in-chief of the Charterless Zarathustra Company or not, and friends like that were hard to come by, once you'd gotten to the top.

Except for Leslie Coombes, he didn't have any friends like that.

Some time during the night, he was awakened by

something soft and warm squirming against his shoulder.

"Hey; I thought I fixed you a bed of your own."

"Yeek?"

"Oh, you want to bunk with Pappy Vic. All right."

They both went back to sleep.

V

It was fun having company for breakfast, especially company small enough to sit on the table. The Fuzzy tasted Grego's coffee; he didn't care for it. He liked fruit juice and sipped some. Then he nibbled Extee-Three, and watched quite calmly while Grego lit a cigarette, but manifested no desire to try one. He'd probably seen humans smoking, and may have picked up a lighted cigarette and either burned himself or hadn't like it.

Grego poured more coffee, and then put on the screen. The Fuzzy turned to look at it. Screens were fun: interesting things happened in them. He was fascinated by the kaleidoscopic jumble of color. Then it cleared, and Myra Fallada appeared in it.

"Good morning, Mr. Grego," she started. Then she choked. Her mouth stayed open, and her eyes bulged as though she had just swallowed a glass of hundred-and-fifty-proof rum thinking it iced tea. Her hand rose falteringly to point.

"Mr. Grego! That . . . Is that a *Fuzzy*?"

The Fuzzy was delighted; this was a lot more fun than the man in the blue clothes, last night.

"That's right. I found him making himself at home,

here, last evening." He wondered how many more times he'd have to go over that. "All I can get out of him is yeeks. For all I know, he may be a big stockholder."

After consideration, Myra decided this was a joke. A sacrilegious joke; Mr. Grego oughtn't to make jokes like that about the company.

"Well, what are you going to do with it?"

"Him? Why, if he wants to stay, fix up a place for him here."

"But . . . But it's a Fuzzy!"

The company lost its charter because of Fuzzies. Fuzzies were the enemy, and loyal company people oughtn't to fraternize with them, least of all Mr. Grego.

"Miss Fallada, the Fuzzies were on this planet for a hundred thousand years before the company was ever thought of." Pity he hadn't taken that attitude from the start. "This Fuzzy is a very nice little fellow, who wants to be friends with me. If he wants to stay with me, I'll be very happy to have him." He closed the subject by asking what had come in so far this morning.

"Well, the girls have most of the morning reports from last night processed; they'll be on your desk when you come down. And then . . ."

And then, the usual budget of gripes and queries. He thought most of them had been settled the day before.

"All right; pile it up on me. Has Mr. Coombes called yet?"

Yes. He was going to be busy all day. He would call again before noon, and would be around at cocktail time. That was all right. Leslie knew what he had to do and how to do it. When he got Myra off the screen, he called Chief Steefer.

Harry Steefer didn't have to zip up his tunic or try to look wide awake; he looked that way already. He was a retired Federation Army officer and had a triple row of ribbon on his left breast to prove it.

"Good morning, Mr. Grego." Then he smiled and nodded at the other person in view in his screen. "I see you still have the trespasser."

"Guest, Chief. What's been learned about him?"

"Well, not too much, yet. I have what you gave Captain Lansky last night; he's tabulated all the reports and complaints on this wave of ransackings and petty thefts. A rather imposing list, by the way. Shall I give it to you in full?"

"No; just summarize it."

"Well, it started, apparently, with ransacking in a couple of offices and a ladies' lounge on the eighth level down. No valuables taken, but things tossed around and left in disorder, and candy and other edibles taken. It's been going on like that ever since, on progressively higher levels. There were reports that somebody was in a couple of cafeteria supply rooms, without evidence of entrance."

"Human entrance, that is."

"Yes. Lansky had a couple of detectives look those places over last night; he says that a Fuzzy could have squirmed into all of them. I had reports on all of it as it happened. Incidentally, there was nothing reported for last night, which confirms the supposition that your Fuzzy was responsible for all of it."

"Regular little vest-pocket crime wave, aren't you." He pummeled the Fuzzy gently. "And there was nothing before the night of the sixteenth or below the eighth level down?"

"That's right, Mr. Grego. I wanted to talk to you before I did anything, but there may be a chance that either Dr. Mallin or Dr. Jimenez may know something about it."

"I'll talk to both of them, myself. Dr. Jimenez was over on Beta until a day or so before the trial; after he'd trapped the four Dr. Mallin was studying, he stayed on to study the Fuzzies in habitat. He had a couple of men helping him, paid hunters or rangers or something of the sort."

"I'll find out who they were," Steefer said. "And, of course, almost anybody who works out of Company House on Beta Continent may have picked the Fuzzy up and brought him back and let him get away. We'll do all we can to find out about this, Mr. Grego."

He thanked Steefer and blanked the screen, and punched out the call-combination of Leslie Coombes' apartment. Coombes, in a dressing gown, answered at once; he was in his library, with a coffee service and a stack of papers in front of him. He smiled and greeted Grego; then his eyes shifted, and the smile broadened.

"Well! Touching scene; Victor Grego and his Fuzzy. If you can't lick them, join them," he commented. "When and where did you pick him up?"

"I didn't; he joined me." He told Coombes about it. "What I want to find out now is who brought him here."

"My advice is, have him flown back to Beta and turned loose in the woods where he came from. Rainsford agreed not to prosecute us for what we did before the trial, but if he finds you're keeping a Fuzzy at Company House now, he'll throw the book at you."

"But he likes it here. He wants to stay with Pappy Vic. Don't you, kid?" he asked. The Fuzzy said something that sounded like agreement. "Suppose you go to Pendarvis and make application for papers of guardianship for me, like the ones he gave Holloway and George Lunt and Rainsford."

A gleam began to creep into Leslie Coombes' eyes. He'd like nothing better than a chance at a return bout with Gus Brannhard, with a not-completely-hopeless case.

"I believe I could . . ." Then he banished temptation. "No; we have too much on our hands now, without another Fuzzy trial. Get rid of him, Victor." He held up a hand to forestall a protest. "I'll be around for cocktails, about 1730-ish," he said, "You think it over till then."

Well, maybe Leslie was right. He agreed, and for a while they talked about the political situation. The Fuzzy became bored and jumped down from the table. After they blanked their screens he looked around and couldn't see him. The door to the pantry-storeroom-toolroom-junkroom was open; maybe he was in there investigating things. That was all right; he couldn't make the existing mess any worse. Grego poured more coffee and lit another cigarette.

There was a loud crash from beyond the open door, and an alarmed yeek, followed by more crashing and thumping and Fuzzy cries of distress. Jumping to his feet, he ran to the door and looked inside.

The Fuzzy was in the middle of a puddle of brownish gunk that had spilled from an open five-gallon can which seemed to have fallen from a shelf. Sniffing, he recognized it — a glaze for baked meats, mostly molasses, that the chef had mixed from a recipe of his own. It took about a pint to glaze a whole ham, so the damned fool had mixed five gallons of it. Most of it had gone on the Fuzzy, and in attempting to get away from the deluge he had upset a lot of jars of spices and herbs, samples of which were sticking to his fur. Then he had put his foot on a sheet of paper, and it had stuck; trying to pull it loose, it had stuck to his hands, too. As soon as he saw Pappy Vic, he gave a desperate yeek of appeal.

"Yes, yeek yourself." He caught the Fuzzy, who flung both adhesive arms around his neck. "Come on, here; let's get you cleaned up."

Carrying the Fuzzy into the bathroom, he dumped him into the tub, then tore off the hopelessly ruined shirt. Trousers all spotted with the stuff, too; change them when he finished the job. He brought a jar of shampoo soap from the closet and turned on the hot water, tempering it to what he estimated the Fuzzy could stand.

Now, wasn't this a Nifflheim of a business? As if he hadn't anything to do but wash Fuzzies.

He rubbed the soap into the Fuzzy's fur; the Fuzzy first resented and then decided he liked it, shrieked in pleasure, and grabbed a handful of the soap and tried to shampoo Grego. Finally, they got finished with it. The Fuzzy liked the hot-air dryer, too. He'd never had a shampoo before.

His fur clean and dry and fluffy, he sat on the bed and watched Pappy Vic change clothes. It was amazing the way the Big Ones could change their outer skins; must be very convenient. He made remarks, from time to time, and Grego carried on a conversation with him.

After he had dressed, Grego recorded a message for the houseboy, to be passed on to the chef and the gardener, to get everything to Nifflheim out of that back room that didn't belong there, and to keep what little did in some kind of decent order. If that place could be kept in order, now, the Fuzzy had one positive accomplishment to his credit.

They took the lift down to the top executive level —

lifts appeared to be a new experience for the Fuzzy, too
— and into his private office. The Fuzzy looked around in
wonder, especially at the big globe of Zarathustra, floating six feet off the floor on its own built-in contragravity
unit, spotlighted from above to simulate Zarathustra's
KO-class sun, its two satellites circling around it. Finally,
for a better view, he jumped up on a chair.

"If I had any idea you'd stay there..." He flipped
the screen switch and got Myra on it. "I had a few things
to clean up before I could come down," he told her, with
literal truthfulness. "How many girls have we in the
front office, this morning?"

There were eight, and they were all busy. Myra started
to tell him what with; maybe four could handle it at a
pinch, and six without undue strain. That was another
thing the Charterless Zarathustra Company would have
to economize on.

"Well, they can look after the Fuzzy, too," he said.
"Take turns with him. He's in here, trying to make up
his mind what kind of deviltry to get into next. Come
get him, and take him out and tell the girls to keep him
innocently amused."

"But, Mr. Grego; they have work..."

"This is more work. We'll find out which one gets
along best with him, and promote her to chief Fuzzy-
sitter. Are we going to let one Fuzzy disrupt our whole
organization?"

Myra started to remind him of what the Fuzzies had
done to the company already, then said, "Yes, Mr.
Grego," and blanked the screen. A moment later she
entered.

She and the Fuzzy looked at one another in mutual
hostility and suspicion. She took a hesitant step forward;
the Fuzzy yeeked angrily, dodged when she reached for

him, and ran to Grego, jumping onto his lap.

"She won't hurt you," he soothed. "This is Myra; she likes Fuzzies. Don't you, Myra?" He stroked the Fuzzy. "I'm afraid he doesn't like you."

"Well, that makes it mutual," Myra said. "Mr. Grego, I am your secretary. I am not an animal keeper."

"Fuzzies are not animals. They are sapient beings. The Chief Justice himself said so. Have you never heard of the Pendarvis Decisions?"

"Have I heard of anything else, lately? Mr. Grego, how you can make a pet of that little demon, after all that's happened . . ."

"All right, Myra. I'll take him."

He went through Myra's office and into the big room they called executive operations center, through which reports from all over the company's shrunken but still extensive empire reached him and his decisions and directives and orders and instructions were handed down to his subjects. There were eight girls there, none particularly busy. One was reading alternately from several sets of clipboarded papers and talking into a vocowriter. Another was making a subdued clatter with a teleprint machine. A third was at a drawing board, constructing one of those multicolored zigzag graphs so dear to the organizational heart. The rest sat smoking and chatting; they all made hasty pretense of busying themselves as he entered. Then one of them saw the Fuzzy in his arms.

"Look! Mr. Grego has a Fuzzy!"

"Why, it's a real live Fuzzy!"

Then they were all on their feet and crowding forward in a swirl of colored dresses and perfumes and eager, laughing voices and pretty, smiling faces.

"Where did you get him, Mr. Grego?"

"Oh, can we see him?"

"Yes, girls." He set the Fuzzy down on the floor. "I don't know where he came from, but I think he wants to stay with us. I'm going to leave him here for a while. Don't let him interfere too much with your work, but keep an eye on him and don't let him get into any trouble. It'll be at least an hour before I have anything ready to go out. You can give him anything you'd eat yourselves; if he doesn't want, he won't take it. I don't think he's very hungry right now. And don't kill him with affection."

When he went out, they were all sitting on the floor in a circle around the Fuzzy, who has having a wonderful time. He told Myra to leave the doors of her office open so he could go through when he wanted to. Then he went through another door, into the computer room.

It was quarter-circular; two straight walls twenty feet long at right angles and the curved wall between, the latter occupied by the input board for the situation-analysis and operation-guidance computers. This was a band of pale green plastic, three feet wide, divided into foot squares by horizontal and vertical red lines, each square perforated with thousands of tiny holes, in some of them, little plug-in lights twinkled in every color of the spectrum. Three levels down, a whole floor was occupied with the computers this board serviced. From it, new information was added in the quasi-mathematical symbology computers understood.

He stood for a moment, looking at the Christmas-tree lights. Nothing in the world would have tempted him to touch it; he knew far too little about it. He wondered if they had started the computers working on the sunstone-buying policy problem, then went out into his own office, closing the door behind him, and sat down at his desk.

In the old, pre-Fuzzy days, he would have spent a leisurely couple of hours here, drinking more coffee and going over reports. Once in a while he would have made some comment, or asked a question, or made a suggestion, to show that he was keeping up with what was going on. Only rarely would any situation arise requiring his personal action.

Now everybody was having situations; things he had thought settled at the marathon staff conference of the past four days were coming unstuck; conflicts were developing. He had to make screen-calls to people he would never have bothered talking to under ordinary circumstances — the superintendent of the meat-packing plant on Delta Continent, the chief engineer on the now-idle Big Blackwater drainage project, the master mechanic at the nuclear-electric power-unit plant. He welcomed one such necessity, the master mechanic at the electronics-equipment factory; they were starting production of ultrasonic hearing-aids for the Government, and he ordered half a dozen sent around to his office. When he got one of them, he could hear what his new friend was saying.

Myra Fallada came in, dithering in the doorway till he had finished talking to the chief of chemical industries about a bottleneck in blasting-explosive production. As soon as he blanked the screen, she began.

"Mr. Grego, you will simply have to get that horrid creature out of operations center. The girls aren't doing a bit of work, and the noise is driving me simply *mad!*"

He could hear shrieks of laughter, and the running scamper of Fuzzy feet. Now that he thought of it, he had been hearing that for some time.

"And I positively can't work ... *Aaaaaa!*"

Something bright red hit her on the back of the head and bounced into the room. A red plastic bag, a sponge bag or swimsuit bag or something like that, stuffed with tissue paper. The Fuzzy ran into the room, dodging past Myra, and hurled it back, within inches of her face, then ran after it.

"Well, yes, Myra. I'm afraid this is being carried a bit far." He rose and went past her into her office, in time to see the improvised softball come whizzing at him from the big office beyond. He caught it and went on through; the Fuzzy ran ahead of him to a tall girl with red hair who stooped and caught him up.

"Look, girls," he said, "I said keep the Fuzzy amused; I didn't say turn this into a kindergarten with the teacher gone AWOL. It's bad enough to have the Fuzzies tear up our charter, without letting them stop work on what we have left."

"Well, it did get a little out of hand," the tall redhead understated.

"Yes. Slightly." Nobody was going to under-understate him. What was her name? Sandra Glenn. "Sandra, he seems to like you. You take care of him. Just keep him quiet and keep him from bothering everybody else."

He hoped she wouldn't ask him how. She didn't; she just said, "I'll try, Mr. Grego." He decided to settle for that; that was all anybody could do.

By the time he got back to his desk, there was a call from the head of Public Services, wanting to know what he was going to tell the school teachers about their job futures. When he got rid of that, he called Dr. Ernst Mallin at Science Center.

The acting head of Science Center was fussily neat in an uncompromisingly black and white costume which matched his uncompromisingly black and white mind. He had a narrow face and a small, tight mouth; it had been an arrogantly positive face once. Now it was the face of a man who expects the chair he is sitting on to collapse under him at any moment.

"Good morning, Mr. Grego." Apprehensive, and trying not to show it.

"Good morning, Doctor. Those Fuzzies you were working with before the trial; the ones Dr. and Mrs. van Riebeek have now. Were they the only ones you had?"

The question took Mallin by surprise. They were, he stated positively. And to the best of his knowledge Juan Jimenez, who had secured them for him, had caught no others.

"Have you talked to Dr. Jimenez yet?" he asked, after hearing about the Fuzzy in Company House. "I don't believe he brought any when he came in from Beta Continent."

"No, not yet. I wanted to talk to you, first, about the Fuzzy and about something else. Dr. Mallin, I gather you're not exactly happy in charge of Science Center."

"No, Mr. Grego. I took it over because it was the only thing to do at the time, but now that the trial is over, I'd much rather go back to my own work."

"Well, so you shall, and your salary definitely won't suffer because of it. And I want to assure you again of my complete confidence in you, Doctor. During the Fuzzy trouble you did the best any man could have, in a thoroughly impossible situation . . ."

He watched the anxiety ebb out of Mallin's face; before he was finished, the psychologist was smiling one of his tight little smiles.

"Now, there's the matter of your successor. What would you think of Juan Jimenez?"

Mallin frowned. Have to make a show of thinking it over, and he was one of these people who thought with his face.

"He's rather young, but I believe it would be a good choice, Mr. Grego. I won't presume to speak of his ability as a scientist, his field is rather far from mine. But he has executive ability, capacity for decisions and for supervision, and gets along well with people. Yes; I should recommend him." He paused, then asked, "Do you think he'll accept it?"

"What do you think, Doctor?"

Mallin chuckled. "That was a foolish question," he admitted. "Mr. Grego; this Fuzzy. You still have him at Company House? What are you going to do with him?"

"Well, I had hoped to keep him, but I'm afraid I can't. He is a little too enterprising. He made my apartment look like a slightly used battlefield this morning, and now he's turning the office into a three-ring circus. And Leslie Coombes advises me to get rid of him; he thinks it may start Rainsford after us again. I think I'll have him taken back to Beta and liberated there."

"I'd like to have him, myself, Mr. Grego. Just keep him at my home and play with him and talk to him and try to find how he thinks about things. Mr. Grego, those Fuzzies are the sanest people I have ever seen. I know; I tried to drive the ones I had psychotic with frustration-situation experiments, and I simply couldn't. If we could learn their basic psychological patterns, it would be the greatest advance in psychology and psychiatry since Freud."

He meant it. He was a different Ernst Mallin now; ready to learn, to conquer his own ignorance instead of denying it. But what he wanted was out of the question.

"I'm sorry, believe me I am. But if I gave you the Fuzzy, Leslie Coombes would have a fit, and that's nothing to what Ben Rainsford would have; he'd bring prosecutions against the lot of us. If I do keep him, you'll have opportunity to study him, but I'm afraid I can't."

He brought the conversation to a close, and blanked the screen. The noise had stopped in operation center; the work probably had, too. He didn't want to get rid of the Fuzzy. He was a nice little fellow. But...

VI

HE WASN'T able to get Juan Jimenez immediately. Juan was doing something at the zoo, and the zoo was spread over too much area to track him down. He left word to call him as soon as possible, and went back to his own work, and finally had his lunch brought in and ate it at the desk. The outside office got noisy again, for a while. The girls seemed to be feeding the Fuzzy, and he wondered apprehensively on what. Some of the things those girls ate would give a billygoat indigestion. About an hour afterward, Jimenez was on the screen.

The chief mammalogist was a young man, with one of those cheerful, alert, agreeable, sincere and accommodating faces you saw everywhere on the upper echelons of big corporations or institutions. He might or might not be a good scientist, but he was a real two-hundred-proof company man.

"Hello, Juan; calling from Science Center?"

"Yes, Mr. Grego. I was at the zoo; they have some new panzer pigs from Gamma. When I got back, they told me you wanted to talk to me."

"Yes. When you came back, just before the trial, from Beta, did you bring any Fuzzies along with you?"

"Good Lord, no!" Jimenez was startled. "I got the impression that we needed Fuzzies like we needed a hole in the head. I got the impression that the one was about equal to the other."

"Just like Ernst Mallin: the more you saw of them, the more sapient they looked. Well, dammit, what else were they? What were you doing on Beta?"

"Well, as I told you, Mr. Grego, we had a camp and we'd attracted about a dozen of them around it with Extee-Three, and we were photographing them and studying behavior, but we never made any attempt to capture any, after the first four."

"Beside yourself, who were 'we'?"

"The two men helping me, a couple of rangers from Survey Division; their names were Herckerd and Novaes. They helped me live-trap the four I gave to Dr. Mallin, and they helped with the camp work, and with photographing and so on."

"Well, here's the situation." He went into it again, realizing why witnesses in court who have been taken a dozen times over their stories by the police and the prosecuting attorney's people always sounded so glib. "So, you see, I want to find out what this is. It may be something quite innocent, but I want to be sure."

"Well, I didn't bring him in, and Herckerd and Novaes came in along with me; they didn't."

"I wish you, or they, had brought him; then I'd know what this is all about. Oh, another thing, Juan. As you know, Dr. Mallin was only in temporary charge at Science Center after Kellogg was arrested. He's going back to what's left of his original job, most happily, I might add. Do you think you could handle it? If you do, you can have it."

One thing you had to give Jimenez, he wasn't a hypocrite. He didn't pretend to be overcome with the honor, and he didn't question his own fitness. "Why, thank you, Mr. Grego!" Then he went into a little speech of acceptance which sounded suspiciously premeditated. Yes; he would definitely accept. So Grego made a little speech of his own, ending:

"I suggest you contact Dr. Mallin at once. He knows of my decision to appoint you, and you'll find him quite pleased to turn over to you. Oh, suppose we have lunch together tomorrow; by that time you should know what you have, and we can talk over future plans."

As soon as he had Jimenez off the screen he got Harry Steefer onto it.

"Mallin says he knows nothing about it, and so does Juan Jimenez. I have the names of two men who were helping Jimenez on Beta . . ."

Steefer grinned. "Phil Novaes and Moses Herckerd; they both worked for the Survey Division. Herckerd's a geologist, and Novaes is a hunter and wildlife man. They came in along with Jimenez the day before the trial, and then they vanished. A company aircar vanished along with them. My guess is they either went prospecting or down into the veldbeest country to do a little rustling. Want me to put out a wanted for them?"

"Yes, do that, Chief, about the car. Too many company vehicles have been vanishing along with employees since this turned into a Class-IV planet. And I still want to know who brought that Fuzzy here—and why."

"We're working on it," Steefer said. "There are close to a hundred people in half a dozen divisions who might have been over on Beta, in Fuzzy country, and picked up a Fuzzy for a pet. Then, say the Fuzzy got away here in Company House. Whoever was responsible would keep quiet about it afterward. I'm trying to find out, but you said you wanted it done discreetly."

"As discreetly as possible; I want it done, though. And you might start a search on some of the unoccupied floors on the eighth and ninth levels down, for evidence of where the Fuzzy was kept before he got away."

Steefer nodded. "We haven't any more men than we need," he mentioned. "Well, I'll do the best I can."

On past performance, Harry Steefer's best was likely to be pretty good. He nodded, satisfied, and went back to work, trying to figure what sort of a cargo could be scraped up for the Terra-Baldur-Marduk liner *City of Kapstaad,* which would be getting in in a week. He was still at it, calculating values on the Terra market against cubic feet of hold-space, when the door from the computer room opened behind him.

He turned, to see Sandra Glenn in the doorway. Her red hair and lipstick and her green eyes were vivid against a face that was white as paper.

"Mr. Grego." It was a barely audible whisper, shocked and frightened. "Were you doing anything with the board?"

"Good God, no!" He shoved his chair back and came to his feet. "I keep my ignorant fingers off that. What's been done to it?"

She stepped forward and aside and pointed. When he looked he saw the middle of the board a blaze of many-colored lights; not the random-looking pattern that would make sense only to a computer or a computerman, but a studied design, symmetrical and harmonious. A beautiful design. But God—Allah to Zeus, take your pick—only knew what gibbering nonsense it was putting into the trusting innards of that computer. Sandra was close to the screaming meemies; she had some idea of what kind of a computation would emerge.

"That," he said, "was our little friend *Fuzzy fuzzy holloway*. He came in here and saw the lights and found out they could be pulled out and shifted around, and he decided to make a real pretty thing. Weren't you, or any of the other girls, watching him?"

"Well, I had some work, and Gertrude was watching him, and then he lay down for a nap after lunch, and somebody called Gertrude to the screen . . ."

"All right. You're not the first one to be fooled by a Fuzzy, and neither's Gertrude. They fooled a guy named Grego pretty badly a few times. Has anything been done about this?"

"No; I just saw it a moment ago . . ."

"All right. Call Joe Verganno. No; I'll do it, his screen girl won't try to argue with me. You go find that Fuzzy."

He crossed in two long steps to the communication screen and punched a combination from the card taped up beside it. The girl who answered started to say, "Master computerman's office," and then saw who she had on screen. "Why, Mr. Grego!"

"Give me Verganno, quick."

Her hand moved; the screen exploded into a shatter of light and cleared with the computerman looking out of it.

"Joe, hell's to pay," he said, before Verganno could speak. "Somebody shoved a lot of plugs into the input board here and bitched everything up. Here." He reached under the screen and grabbed something that looked vaguely like a pistol, with a wide-angle lens where the muzzle should be, connected with the screen by a length of minicable. Aiming at the colored pattern on the board, he squeezed the trigger switch. Behind him, Joe Verganno's voice howled:

"Good God! Who did that?"

"A Fuzzy. No, I'm not kidding; that's right. You got it?"

"Just a sec. Yeah, turn it off." In the screen, Verganno grabbed a handphone. "General warning, all computer outlets. False data has been added affecting Executive One and Executive Two; no reliance is to be placed on computations from Executive One or Two until further notice. All right, Mr. Grego, I'll be right up. You mean there's a Fuzzy loose in your office?"

"Yes, he's been here all day. I don't think," he added, "that he'll be here much longer."

One of the girls looked into the room from operation-center.

"We can't find him anywhere, Mr. Grego!" she almost wailed. "And it's all my fault; I was supposed to be watching him!"

"Hell with whose fault it is; find him. If it's anybody's fault it's mine for bringing him here."

That was a fault that would be rectified directly. He saw Myra dithering in the door of her office.

"Get Ernst Mallin. Tell him to come here and get that damned Fuzzy to Nifflheim out of here."

Argue about the legal aspects later; if Mallin wanted a Fuzzy to study, he could have one. Myra said something about better late than never, and retracted into her office. The door from the outside hall opened cautiously, and a couple of police and three mechanics from one of the aircar hangars entered; somebody's had sense enough to call for reinforcements. One of the mechanics had a blanket over his arm; that was smart, too. The girls were searching the big room, and keeping watch on the doors. The hall door opened again, and Joe Verganno and one of his technicians came in with a hand lifter loaded with tools.

"Anything been done to the board yet?" he asked.

"Nifflheim, no! We're not making a bad matter worse than it is. See if you can figure out what's happening in the computer."

"A couple of my men are going to find that out down below. Lemme see this screen, now." He went into the room, followed by the technician with the lifter. The technician said something obscenely blasphemous a moment later.

He went back to the big room; through the open door of her office, he could hear Myra talking to somebody. "Come and get him, right away. No, we don't know where he is . . . *Eeeeeeh!* Get away from me, you little monster! Mr. Grego, here he is!"

"Grab him and hold him," he ordered. "Go help her," he told one of the cops. "Don't hurt the Fuzzy; just get hold of him."

Then he turned and ran through the computer room almost colliding with Verganno's helper, and ran into his own office. As he skidded around his desk, the Fuzzy dashed through the door of Myra's office. The blanket the aircar mechanic had been carrying sailed after him, missing him. Myra, the cop, and the mechanic came running after it; the mechanic caught his feet in it and went down. The cop tripped over him, and Myra tripped over the cop. The cop was cursing. Myra was screaming. The mechanic, knocked breathless under both of them, was merely gasping. The Fuzzy landed on top of the desk, saw Grego, and took off from there, landing against his chest and throwing his arms around Grego's neck. One of the girls, coming through from Myra's office and avoiding the struggling heap in front of the door,

66

whooped, "Come on, everybody! Mr. Grego's caught him!"

The cop, who had gotten to his feet, said, "I'll take him, Mr. Grego," and reached for the Fuzzy. The Fuzzy yeeked loudly, and clung tighter to Grego.

"No, I'll hold him. He isn't afraid of me." He sat down in his desk chair, holding the Fuzzy and stroking him. "It's all right, kid. Nobody's going to hurt you. And we're going to take you out of here, to a nice place where you can have fun, and people'll be good to you..."

The words meant nothing to the Fuzzy; the voice, and the stroking hands, were comforting and reassuring. He snuggled closer, making happy little sounds. He was safe, now.

"What are you gonna do with him, Mr. Grego?" the cop asked.

Grego hugged the Fuzzy to him. "I'm not going to do anything with him. Look at him; he trusts me; he thinks I won't let anybody do anything to him. Well, I won't. I never let anybody who trusted me down yet, and be damned if I'll start now, with a Fuzzy."

"You mean, you're going to keep him?" Myra demanded. "After what he did?"

"He didn't mean to do anything bad, Myra. He just wanted to make a pretty thing with the lights. I'll bet he's as proud as anything of it. It's just going to be up to me to see that he doesn't get at anything else he can make trouble with."

"Dr. Mallin said he was coming right away. He'll be disappointed."

"He'll have to be disappointed, then. He can study the Fuzzy here. And get the building superintendent and the chief decorator; tell them I want them to start putting in a Fuzzy garden up on my terrace. Tell both of them to come up to my suite personally; tell them I want work started immediately, and I'll authorize double time for overtime till it's finished."

The Fuzzy wasn't scared, any more. Pappy Vic was taking care of him. And all these other Big Ones were listening to Pappy Vic; they wouldn't hurt him or chase him any more.

"And call Tregaskis at Electronics Equipment; ask him what's holding up those hearing-aids he was going to send me. And I'll need somebody to help look after the kid. Sandra, do you do anything we can't replace you at? Then you've just been appointed Fuzzy Sitter in Chief. You start immediately; ten percent raise as of this morning.

Sandra was happy. "I'll love that, Mr. Grego. What's his name?"

"Name? I don't have a name for him, yet. Anybody have any ideas?"

"I have a few!" Myra said savagely.

"Call him Diamond," Joe Verganno, in the doorway of the computer room, suggested.

"Because he's so small and precious? I like that. But don't be a piker. Call him Sunstone."

"No; that was probably why the original Diamond was named, but I was thinking of calling him after a little dog that belonged to Sir Isaac Newton," Verganno said. "It seems Diamond got hold of a manuscript Sir Isaac had just finished and was going to send to his publisher. Mostly math, all done with a quill pen, no carbons of course. So Diamond got this manuscript down on the floor and he tore hell out of it, which meant about three months' work to do over. When Newton saw it, he just looked at it, and then sat down with the dog on his lap, and said, 'Oh, Diamond, poor Diamond; how little you know what mischief you have done!' "

"That's a nice little story, Joe. It's something I'll want to remind myself of, now and then. Bet you'll give a lot of reasons to, won't you, Diamond?"

VII

JACK HOLLOWAY leaned back in his chair, resting one ankle across the corner of the desk and propping the other foot on a partly open bottom drawer. If he had to work in an office, it was nice working in a real one, and it was a big improvement to be able to use his living quarters exclusively for living in again. The wide doors at either end of the arched prefab hut were open and a little breeze was drawing through, just enough to keep the place cool and carry off his pipe smoke. There wasn't so much noise outside any more; most of the new buildings were up now. He could hear a distant popping of small arms as the dozen and a half ZNPF recruits fired for qualification.

A hundred yards away, at the other end, Sergeant Yorimitsu was monitoring screen-views transmitted in from a couple of cars up on patrol, and Lieutenant Ahmed Khadra and Sergeant Knabber were taking the fingerprints of a couple of Fuzzies that had come in an hour ago. Little Fuzzy, resting the point of his chopper-digger on the floor with his hands on the knob pommel, watched boredly. Fingerprinting was old stuff, now. The space between was mostly vacant; a few unoccupied desks

70

and idle business machines scattered about. Some of these days they'd have a real office force, and then he'd be able to get out and move around among the natives, the way a Commissioner ought to.

One thing, they had the Fuzzy Reservation question settled, at least for now. Ben Rainsford was closing everything north of the Little Blackwater and the East Fork of the Snake to settlement; that country all belonged to the Fuzzies and nobody else. Now if the Fuzzies could only be persuaded to stay there. And Gerd and Ruth and Pancho Ybarra and the Andrews girl were here, now, and set up. Maybe they'd begin to find out a few of the things they had to know.

The stamp machine banged twice, putting numbers on the ID discs for the two newcomers. Khadra brought the discs back and squatted to put them on the two Fuzzies.

"How many is that, now, Ahmed?" he called down the hut.

"These are Fifty-eight and Fifty-nine," Khadra called back. "Deduct three, two for Rainsford's, and one for Goldilocks."

Poor little Goldilocks; she'd have loved having an ID disc. She'd been so proud of the little jingle-charm Ruth had given her, just before she'd been killed. Fifty-six Fuzzies; getting quite a population here.

The communication screen buzzed. He flipped a switch on the edge of his desk and dropped his feet to the floor, turning. It was Ben Rainsford, and he was furiously angry about something. His red whiskers bristled as though electrically charged, and his blue eyes were almost shooting sparks.

"Jack," he began indignantly, "I've just found out that Victor Grego has a Fuzzy cooped up at Company House. What's more, he's had the effrontery to have Leslie

Coombes apply to Judge Pendarvis to have him appointed guardian."

That surprised him slightly. To date, Grego hadn't exactly established himself as one of the Friends of Little Fuzzy.

"How did he get him, do you know?"

Rainsford gobbled in rage for a moment, then said:

"He claims he found this Fuzzy in his apartment, night before last, up at the top of Company House. Now isn't that one Nifflheim of a story; does he think anybody's silly enough to believe that?"

"Well, it is a funny place for a Fuzzy to be," he admitted. "You suppose it might be one that was live-apped for Mallin to study, before the trial? Ruth says ere were only four, and they were all turned loose the ight of the Lurkin business."

"I don't know. All I know is what Gus Brannhard told me that Pendarvis' secretary told him, that Pendarvis told her, that Coombes told Pendarvis." That sounded pretty roundabout, but he supposed that was the way Colonial Governors had to get things. "Gus says Coombes claims Grego says he doesn't know where the Fuzzy came from or how he got into Company House. That is probably a thumping big lie."

"It's probably the truth. Victor Grego's too smart to lie to his lawyer, and Coombes is too smart to lie to the Chief Justice. Judges are funny about that; they want statements veridicated, and after what you saw happen to Mallin in court, you don't suppose any of that crowd would try to lie under veridication."

Rainsford snorted scornfully. Grego was lying; if the veridicator backed him up, the veridicator was as big a liar as he was.

"Well, I don't care how he got the Fuzzy; what I'm

concerned with is what he's doing to him," Rainsford replied. "And Ernst Mallin; Coombes admitted to Pendarvis that Mallin was helping Grego look after the Fuzzy. *Look after* him! They're probably torturing the poor thing, Grego and that sadistic quack head-shrinker. Jack, you've got to get that Fuzzy away from Grego!"

"Oh, I doubt that. Grego wouldn't mistreat the Fuzzy, and if he was, he wouldn't apply for papers of guardianship and make himself legally responsible. What do you want me to do?"

"Well, I told Gus to get a court order; Gus told me you were the Native Commissioner, that it was your job to act to protect the Fuzzy..."

Gus didn't think the Fuzzy needed any protecting; he thought Grego was treating him well, and ought to be allowed to keep him. So he'd passed the buck. He nodded.

"All right. I'm coming in to Mallorysport now. You're three hours behind us here, and if I use Gerd's boat I can make it in three hours. I'll be at Government House at 1530, your time. I'll bring either Pancho or Ruth along. You have Gus meet us when we get in. And I'll want to borrow your Flora and Fauna."

"What for?"

"Interpreters, and to interrogate Grego's Fuzzy. And I want them instead of any of our crowd here because they may have to testify in court and they won't have to travel back and forth. And tell Gus to get all the papers we'll need to crash Company House with. This is the first time anything like this has come up. We're going to give it the full treatment."

He blanked the screen, scribbled on a notepad and tore off the sheet, then looked around. Ko-Ko and Cinderella and Mamma Fuzzy and a couple of the Constabulary Fuzzies were working on a jigsaw puzzle on the floor near his desk.

"Ko-Ko," he called. *"Do-bizzo."* When Ko-Ko got to his feet and came over, he handed him the note. "Give to Unka Panko," he said. "Make run fast."

Victor Grego had Leslie Coombes on screen; the lawyer was saying:

"The Chief Justice is not hostile. Hospitable, I'd say. I think he's trying to be careful not to establish any precedent that might embarrass the Native Affairs Commission later. He was rather curious about how the Fuzzy got into Company House, though."

"Tell him that makes two of us. So am I."

"Have Steefer's men found out anything yet?"

"Not that he's reported. I'm going to talk to him shortly. The way things are, he's spread out pretty thin."

"It would help a lot if we could explain that. Would you be willing to make a veridicated statement of what you know?"

"With adequate safeguards. Not for anybody to pump me about business matters."

"Naturally. How about Mallin and Jimenez?"

"They will if they want to keep on working for the company." It surprised him that Coombes would even ask such a question. "You think it's necessary?"

"I think it very advisable. Rainsford will certainly oppose your application; possibly Holloway. How about getting a statement from the Fuzzy?"

"Mallin and I tried, last evening. I don't know any of the language, and he only has a few tapes he got from Lieutenant Ybarra at the time of the trial. We have hearing-aids, now. It's a hell of a language; sounds like

Old Terran Japanese more than anything else. The Fuzzy was trying to tell us something, but we couldn't make out what. We have it all on tape.

"And we showed him audio-visual portraits of those two Survey rangers who were helping Jimenez. He made both of them; I doubt if he likes them very much. We're looking for them. We are also looking for a Company scout car that vanished along with them."

"Vehicle theft's a felony; that will do to hold and interrogate them on," Coombes mentioned. "Well, shall I see you for cocktails?"

"Yes. You'd better call me, say every half-hour. If Rainsford gets nasty about this, I may need you before then."

After that, he called Chief Steefer. Steefer greeted him with:

"Mr. Grego, how red is my face?"

"Not noticeably so. Should it be?"

Steefer swore. "Mr. Grego, I want your authorization to make an inch-by-inch search of this whole building."

"Good God, Harry!" He was thinking of how many millions on millions of inches that was. "Have you found something?"

"Not about the Fuzzy, but—You have no idea what's been going on here, on these unoccupied levels. We found places where people had been camping for weeks. We found one place where there must have been a non-stop party going on for a month; there was almost a lifter scow full of empty bottles. And we found a tea pad."

"Yes? What was that like?"

"Nothing much; lot of mattresses thrown around, and the floor covered with butts—mostly chuckleweed or opiate-impregnated tobacco. I don't think that was any of our people; everybody and his girl friend in Mallorysport seems to have been sneaking in here. We have men at all the landing stages, of course, but there aren't enough to . . ." His face hardened. "I've just gone slack on the job. That's the only explanation I can make."

"We've all gone slack, Harry." He thought of the mess in his pantry; that was symptomatic. "You know, we may owe the Fuzzies a debt of gratitude, if what's happened to us will make us start acting like a business concern instead of a bunch of kids in fairyland. All right; go ahead. Finding out how the Fuzzy got in here is still of top importance, but clean house generally while you're at it and see that it stays cleaned up."

Then he called Juan Jimenez at Science Center. Jimenez had gotten a new suit since yesterday, less casual, more executive. His public face had been done over too, to emphasize efficiency rather than agreeableness.

"Good morning, Victor." He stumbled a little over the first name, which was a prerogative of a division chief but to which he was not yet accustomed.

"Good morning, Juan. I know you haven't forgotten we're lunching together, but I wondered if you could make it a little early. There are a couple of things we want to go over first. In twenty minutes?"

"Easily; sooner than that if you wish."

"As soon as you can make it. Just come in the back way."

Then he made another screen call. This was an outside call, for which he had to look up the combination. When the screen cleared, a thin-faced, elderly man with white hair looked out of it. He wore a gray work smock, the breast pockets full of small tools and calibrating instruments. His name was Henry Stenson, and he might have been called an instrument maker, just as Benvenuto Cellini might have been called a jeweler.

"Why, Mr. Grego," he greeted, in pleased surprise, or reasonable facsimile. "I haven't heard from you for some time."

"No. Not since that gadget you planted in my globe stopped broadcasting. Incidentally, the globe's about thirty seconds slow, and both moons are impossibly out of synchronization. We had to stop it to take out that thing you built into it, and none of my people have your fine touch."

Stenson grimaced slightly. "I suppose you know for whom I did that?"

"Well, I'm not certain whether you're Navy Intelligence, like our former employee, Ruth Ortheris, or Colonial Office Investigative Bureau; but that's minor. Whoever, they're to be congratulated on an excellent operative. You know, I could get quite nasty about that; planting radio-transmitted microphones in people's offices is a felony. I don't intend doing anything, but I definitely want no more of it. You can understand my attitude."

"Well, naturally, Mr. Grego. You know," he added, "I thought that thing was detection-proof."

"Instrumentally, yes. My people were awed when they saw the detection-baffles on that thing. Have you patented them? If you have, we owe you some money, because we're copying them. But nothing is proof against physical search, and we practically tore my office apart as soon as it became evident that anything said in it was known almost immediately on Xerxes Base."

Stenson nodded gravely. "You didn't call me just to tell me you'd caught me out? I knew that as soon as the radio went dead."

"No. I want you to put the globe back in synchronization, as soon as possible. And there's another thing.

You helped the people on Xerxes design those ultrasonic hearing-aids, didn't you? Well, could you attack the problem from the other side, Mr. Stenson? I mean, design a little self-powered hand-phone, small enough for a Fuzzy to carry, that would transform the Fuzzy's voice to audible frequencies?"

Stenson was silent for all of five seconds. "Yes, of course, Mr. Grego. If anything, it should be simpler. Of course, teaching the Fuzzy to carry and use it would be a problem, but not in my line of work."

"Well, try and get an experimental model done as soon as possible. I have a Fuzzy available to try it. And if there's anything patentable about it, get it protected. Talk to Leslie Coombes. This may be of commercial value to both of us."

"You think there'll be a demand?" Stenson asked. "How much do you think a Fuzzy would pay for one?"

"I think the Native Affairs Commission would pay ten to fifteen sols apiece for them, and I'm sure our electronics plant could turn them out to sell profitably for that."

Somebody had entered the office; in one of the strategically-placed mirrors, he saw that it was Juan Jimenez keeping out of the field of the screen-pickup. He nodded to him and went on talking to Stenson, who would be around the next morning to look at the globe. When they finished the conversation and blanked screens, he motioned Jimenez to his deskside chair.

"How much of that did you hear?" he asked.

"Well, I heard that white-haired old Iscariot say he'd be around tomorrow to fix the globe . . ."

"Henry Stenson is no Iscariot, Juan. He is a Terran Federation secret agent, and the Federation is to be congratulated on his loyalty and ability. Now that I know

78

just what he is, and now that he knows I know it, we can do business on a friendly basis of mutual respect and distrust. He's going to work up a gadget by which the Fuzzies can speak audibly to us.

"Now, about Fuzzies," he continued. "We're sure that your two helpers, Herckerd and Novaes, brought this Fuzzy of mine here to Mallorysport. You say they didn't have him when they came back with you?"

"Absolutely not, Mr. Grego."

"Would you veridicate that?"

Jimenez didn't want to, that was plain. But he did want to work for the Company, especially now that he had just been promoted to chief of Scientific Study and Research. He was as close to the top of the Company House hierarchy as he could get, and he wanted to stay there.

"Yes, of course. I'd hoped, though, that my word would be good enough . . ."

"Nobody's word's going to be good enough. I'm going to veridicate what I know about it, myself; so's Ernst Mallin. There will be quite a few veridicated statements taken in the next few days. Now, I want you to meet this Fuzzy. See if you know him, or if he knows you."

They went out to the private lift and up to the penthouse. In the living room, Sandra Glenn was lounging in his favorite chair, listening to something from a record-player with an earphone and smoking. As they entered, she shut off the player and closed her eyes. "So-josso-aki; you give me," she said. "Aki-josso-so; I give you. So-noho-aki dokko; you tell me how many."

They tiptoed past her and out onto the terrace. Ernst Mallin was sitting on a low hassock, with his hearing-aid on; Diamond was squatting in front of him, tying knots in a length of twine. An audiovisual recorder was set up to cover both of them. Diamond sprang to his feet and ran to meet them, crying out: "Pappy Vic! *Heeta!*" and holding up the cord to show the knots he had been learning to tie.

"Hello, Diamond. Those are very fine knots. You are a smart Fuzzy. How do I say that, Ernst?" Mallin said something, haltingly; he repeated it, patting the Fuzzy's head. "Now, how do I ask him if he's ever seen this Big One with me before?"

Mallin asked the question himself. Diamond said something; he caught "*Vov,*" a couple of times. That was negative.

"He doesn't know you, Juan. What I'm sure happened is that Herckerd and Novaes came in with you, just before the trial, then went back to Beta, probably in the aircar they stole from us, and picked up this Fuzzy. We won't know why till we catch them and question them." He turned to Mallin. "Get anything more out of him?"

Mallin shook his head. "I'm picking up a few more words, but I still can't be sure. He says two Hagga, the ones we showed him the films of, brought him here. I think they brought some other Fuzzies with him; I can't be sure. There doesn't seem to be any way of pluralizing in his language. He says they were *tosh-ki gashta,* bad people. They put him in a bad place."

"We'll put them in a bad place. Penitentiary place. I don't suppose you can find out how long ago this was? During or right after the trial, I suppose."

Sandra Glenn came out onto the terrace.

"Mr. Grego; Miss Fallada's on screen. She says representatives of all the press-services are here. They've heard about Diamond; they want the story, and pictures of him."

"That was all we needed! All right; tell her to have a

policeman show them up. I'm afraid our lunch'll have to
wait till we get through with them, Juan."

VIII

COMING OUT of the lift, Jack Holloway advanced to let
the others follow and halted, looking at the three men
waiting to meet them in the foyer of Victor Grego's
apartment. Two he had met already: Ernst Mallin, under
uniformly unpleasant circumstances culminating in the
murder of Goldilocks, the beating of Leonard Kellogg
and the shooting of Kurt Borch, at his camp, and Leslie
Coombes, first at George Lunt's complaint court at Beta
Fifteen and then in Judge Pendarvis' court during the
Fuzzy Trial. As the trial had dragged out, the frigid
politeness with which he and Coombes had first met had
thawed into something like mutual cordiality.

But, except for news-screen appearances, he had never
seen Victor Grego before. Enemy generals rarely met
while the fighting was going on. It struck him that,
meeting Grego for the first time as a complete stranger,
he would have instantly liked him. He had to remember
that Grego was the man who had wanted to treat Fuzzies as fur-bearing animals and exterminate the whole
race. Well, Grego hadn't known any Fuzzies, then. It
was easy enough to plan atrocities against verbal labels.

They paused for an instant, ten feet apart, Mallin and

Coombes flanking Grego, and Gus Brannhard, Pancho Ybarra, Ahmed Khadra and Flora and Fauna behind him, like two gangs waiting for somebody to pull a gun. Then Grego stepped forward, extending his hand.

"Mr. Holloway? Happy to meet you." They shook hands. "You've met Mr. Coombes and Dr. Mallin. It was good of you to warn us you were coming."

Ben Rainsford hadn't thought so. He'd wanted them to descend on Company House by surprise, probably with drawn pistols, and catch Grego red-handed at whatever villainy he was up to. Brannhard and Coombes were shaking hands, so were Ybarra and Mallin. He introduced Ahmed Khadra.

"And these other people are Flora and Fauna," he added. "I brought them along to meet Diamond."

Grego stooped, and they came forward. He said, "Hello, Flora; hello, Fauna. *Aki-gazza heeta-so.*"

The accent was reasonably good, but he had to think between words. The two Fuzzies replied politely. Grego started to say that Diamond was out on the terrace, then laughed when he saw the Fuzzy peeping through the door from the living room. An instant later, Diamond saw Flora and Fauna and rushed forward, and they ran to meet him, all jabbering excitedly. A tall girl with red hair entered behind him; Grego introduced her as Sandra Glenn. And behind her came Juan Jimenez; regular Old Home Week.

"Shall we go in the living room, or out on the terrace?" Grego asked. "I'd advise the terrace; the living room might be a little crowded, with three Fuzzies getting acquainted. Sometimes it seems a trifle crowded with just one Fuzzy."

They went through the living room; the quiet and tasteful luxury of its furnishings had suffered somewhat.

There was an audiovisual recorder set up, and an extra reading screen and an audiovisual screen and a tape-player; they looked more like office equipment than domestic furnishings. Evidently Fuzzies did the same things to living rooms everywhere. And another piece of furniture, surprising in any living room; a thing like an old-fashioned electric chair, with a bright metal helmet and a big translucent globe mounted above it. A poly-encephalographic veridicator; Grego wasn't expecting anybody to take his unsupported word about anything. They all affected not to notice it, and passed out onto the terrace.

This had evidently been Grego's private garden; now it seemed to be mostly the Fuzzy's. An awful lot of men must have been working awfully hard up here recently. There was a lot of playground equipment—swing, slide, skeletal construction of jointed pipe for climbing-bars. A little Fuzzy-sized drinking fountain, and a bathing pool. Grego seemed to have just thought of everything he'd like if he were a Fuzzy and gotten it. Diamond led Flora and Fauna to the slide, ran up the ladder, and came shooting down. They both ran after him and tried it, too, and then ran up to try it again. Have to get some playground stuff like that for the camp. Bet Flora and Fauna would start pestering Pappy Ben to get them some things like this, as soon as they got home.

According to plan, Ahmed Khadra and Pancho Ybarra stayed on the terrace with the Fuzzies; he and Gus and Grego and Mallin and Coombes went back inside. For a while, they chatted about Fuzzies in general and Diamond in particular. One thing was obvious: Grego liked Fuzzies, and was devoted to his own.

The Fuzzies had done him all the damage they could. Now he could be friends with them.

"I suppose you want to hear how he turned up, here? If you don't mind, I'd prefer veridicating what I have to tell you, so there won't be any argument about it. Do you want to test the machine first, Mr. Brannhard?"

"It would be a good idea. Jack, you want to be the test witness?"

"If you do the questioning."

A veridicator operated by identifying and registering the distinctive electromagnetic brain-wave pattern involved in suppression of a true statement and substitution of a false one. You didn't have to do that aloud; a mere intention to falsify would turn the blue light in the globe red, and even a yogi adept couldn't control his thoughts enough to prevent it. He took his place in the chair, and Brannhard clipped on the electrodes and lowered the helmet over his head.

"What is your name?"

He answered that truthfully, and Gus nodded and asked him his place of residence.

"How old are you?"

He lied ten years off his age. The veridicator caught that at once; Gus wanted to know how old he really was.

"Seventy-four: I was born in 580. I couldn't even estimate how much to allow for on time-differential for hyperspace trips."

"That's the truth," Gus said. "I didn't think you were much over sixty."

Then he asked about the planets he'd been on. Jack named them, including one he'd never been within fifty light-years of, and the veridicator caught that. He ended in a crimson blaze of mendacity by claiming to be a teetotaler, a Gandhian pacifist, and the illegitimate son of a Satanist archbishop. Brannhard was satisfied; the veridicator worked. He unfastened Jack, and Grego took his place.

The globe stayed blue all through Grego's account of how he had found Diamond in his bedroom; it was the same story they had already gotten from newscasts while coming in from Beta. Then Grego gave place to Mallin, and Mallin to Jimenez. They were all uninvolved in bringing the Fuzzy to Mallorysport, and the veridicator supported them. They all agreed that Diamond had recognized Herckerd and Novaes as the men who had brought him and possibly other Fuzzies there.

"What do you think?" Coombes asked, when they were all back in their chairs. "Do you think they brought those Fuzzies in to sell as pets?"

"I can't see any other reason. I've been expecting something like this. Why would they bring them to Company House, though? I don't quite see the sense in that."

"I do." Grego was angry about something. What he was angry about emerged immediately; he spoke bitterly about what had been going on among the unoccupied rooms of Company House. "Chief Steefer's on the warpath, starting with his own department. We have wants out for Herckerd and Novaes, on a stolen-vehicle charge . . ."

"Forget about that," Brannhard advised. "That's petty larceny to what I'm going to charge them with."

Khadra came in from outside; he took off his beret, but left his pistol on.

"Well, there were six of them," he said. "Diamond, and five others. Herckerd and Novaes—he's positive about the identification—brought them in and kept them for a couple of days in a dark room somewhere in this building. Then the others were taken away; Diamond made a break and got away from the two *tosh-ki Hagga* while they were being put in the aircar. He doesn't know how long ago it was—three sleeps, he says. He found things to eat, and he found water to drink, and then Pappy Vic found him and gave him wonderful-food. He doesn't know what happened to his friends; he hopes they got away too."

"They didn't in here," Grego said. "Are you going to hunt for them?"

"We certainly are."

"And if anything's happened to them, we'll hunt for Herckerd and Novaes till they die of old age if we don't catch them first," Brannhard added.

"How's Diamond like it here, Ahmed?"

"Oh, wonderful. He's the happiest Fuzzy I ever saw, and I never saw any real melancholy Fuzzies. You have a mighty nice Fuzzy, Mr. Grego."

"Well, that's if I'll be allowed to keep him," Grego said.

"My report's going to be very favorable," Khadra told him.

"Of course you will, Mr. Grego. You like the Fuzzy, and he likes you, and he's happy here. That's all I'm interested in."

"I'm afraid Governor Rainsford isn't going to see it like that, Mr. Holloway."

"Governor Rainsford isn't Commissioner of Native Affairs. And he isn't the Federation Courts. The way Judge Péndarvis told me a week ago, the court will accept the advice of the Commission on Fuzzy questions."

"The Attorney-General has a little influence with the court, too," Brannhard said. "The Attorney-General will recommend granting your application for adoption." He rose to his feet. "We don't have anything more to talk

about, do we? Then let's go out and see how the Fuzzies
are doing."

IX

Gus Brannhard poured coffee into a cup already half full of brandy, brushed his beard out of the way with his left hand, and tasted it. It was good, but he still thought it would be better out of a tin pannikin beside a campfire on Beta. It was time to get down to business; after the bare report while hustling indecently through cocktails, they had talked all around the subject at dinner.

"Well, I can and will bring criminal charges," he assured the others who were having coffee in the drawing room at Government House. "Forcible overpowering and transportation under restraint; if that isn't kidnapping what is it?"

"Try your damnedest to make enslavement out of it, Gus," Jack Holloway said. "If you get a conviction, we can have the pair of them shot. And telecast the executions; a real memorable public example is what we want, right now."

"Well, I got the whole story out of Diamond," Pancho Ybarra said. "He and another Fuzzy met four others; the six of them went down a little stream past a waterfall, and then came to a place where there were two

Hagga, the ones he was shown audiovisuals of. The Hagga gave them Extee-Three, and then gave them something out of a bottle. They all woke up with hangovers in what sounds like one of the unfinished rooms in Company House. Diamond got away from them; the two bad Big Ones took the rest away."

"So now we have five Fuzzies to hunt," Holloway said. "That'll be your job, Ahmed. You'll stay here in Mallorysport. We'll promote you to captain and chief of detectives; that'll give you a little status equality with the other enforcement heads around here. If they're trapping Fuzzies for sale, that's not just Native Commission business; that's Federation stuff."

"They probably caught them for Mallin to experiment with," Ben Rainsford said.

Jack swore. "Ben, you haven't been paying attention. All this stuff we got from them was veridicated. They don't know anything about any Fuzzies but those four Gerd and Ruth have."

"Mr. Grego has been cooperating very satisfactorily, Governor," Ahmed Khadra said, stiffly formal. "He has the whole Company police working on it, and told me to call on Chief Steefer for anything, and tomorrow Dr. Jimenez is going out to Beta to show some of our people where he was camping. From the Fuzzy's description, we think Herckerd and Novaes went back there."

"Well, what are you going to do about that Fuzzy at Company House?" he asked Jack, ignoring Khadra's words. "You aren't going to let him stay with Grego, are you?"

"Of course we are. Diamond's happy, and Grego's taking good care of him. I'm going to recommend that Judge Pendarvis issue papers of guardianship to him."

"But it isn't right! Not after all Grego did," Rainsford insisted. "Why, he was going to have all the Fuzzies trapped off for their furs. He took your own Fuzzies away from you. He had Jimenez trap those other four, and let Mallin torture them, ask Ruth about that, and then started the story about the Lurkin girl and turned them loose for the mob to kill. And look how he was trying to make out that you'd just taught your Fuzzies a few tricks and then got me to back up your claim that they were sapient beings..."

There, at last and obliquely, Ben had let the cat out. What he meant was that Grego had tried to accuse him of deliberately engineering a scientific fraud. Well, a scientist would have trouble forgiving that. It was like accusing a soldier of treason or a doctor of malpractice.

"Well, it's my professional opinion," Pancho Ybarra said, "that Grego and Diamond are much attached to each other, and that it would be injustice to both to separate them, and probably psychologically harmful to the Fuzzy. I shall so advise Judge Pendarvis."

"I think that'll be official policy," Holloway said. "When we find Fuzzies and humans living happily together, we have no right to separate them, and we won't."

Rainsford, who had started to fill his pipe, looked up angrily.

"Maybe you forget I'm the Governor; I make the policy. I appointed you..."

Jack's white mustache was twitching at the tips; his eyes narrowed. He looked like an elderly and irascible tiger.

"That's right," he said. "You appointed me Commissioner of Native Affairs. Any time you don't like the way I do my job, get yourself a new Commissioner."

"Get yourself a new Attorney-General, too. I'm with Jack on this."

Rainsford dropped his pipe into the tobacco pouch.

"You mean you're all against me? What are you doing, bucking for jobs with the CZC?"

After a crack like that, there were those who would have insisted on continuing the discussion by correspondence and through seconds. With anybody but Ben Rainsford, he would have, himself. He turned to Pancho Ybarra.

"Doctor, as a psychiatrist what is your opinion of that outburst?" he asked.

"I'm not entitled to express an opinion," the Navy psychologist replied. "Governor Rainsford is not my patient."

"You mean, I ought to be somebody's?" Rainsford demanded.

"Well, now that you ask, you're not exactly psychotic, but you're certainly not displaying much sanity on the subject of Victor Grego."

"You think we ought to just sit back and let him do anything he pleases; run the planet the way he did before the Pendarvis Decisions?"

"He didn't do such a bad job, Ben," he said. "I'm beginning to think he did a damn sight better job than you'll do unless you stop playing Hatfields and McCoys and start governing. You have to arrange for elections for delegates, and a constitutional convention. You have to take over and operate all these public services the Company's been relieved of responsibility for when their charter was invalidated. And you'll have to stop this cattle rustling on Beta and Delta Continents, or you'll have a couple of first-class range wars on your hands. And you'd better start thinking about the immigrant rush that's going to hit this planet when the news of the Pendarvis Decisions gets around."

Rainsford, his pipe and tobacco shoved into his side pocket, was on his feet. He'd tried to interrupt a couple of times.

"Oh, to Nifflheim with you!" he cried. "I'm going out and talk to my Fuzzies."

With that, he flung out of the room. For a moment, nobody said anything, then Jack Holloway swore.

"I hope the Fuzzies talk some sense into him. Be damned if I can."

They probably would, if he'd listen to them. They had more sense than he had, at the moment. Ahmed Khadra, who had sat mumchance through the upper-echelon brawl, clattered his cup and saucer.

"Jack, you think we ought to go check in at the hotel?" he asked.

"Nifflheim, no! This isn't Ben Rainsford's private camp, this is Government House," Holloway said. "We work for the Government, too. We have work to do now."

"We'll have to talk to him again." He wasn't looking forward to it with any pleasure. "We have to get some kind of a Fuzzy Code scotchtaped together, and he'll have to okay it. We need special legislation, and till we can get a Colonial Legislature, that'll have to be by executive decree. And you'll have to figure out a way to make Fuzzies available for adoption. You can't break up a black market by shooting a few people for enslavement; you'll have to make it possible for people to get Fuzzies legally, with controls and safeguards, instead of buying them from racketeers."

"I know it, Gus," Jack said. "I've been thinking about it; a regular adoption bureau. But who can I get to handle it? I don't know anybody."

"Well, I know everybody around Central Courts Building." That ought to be enough; Central Courts was like a village, in which everybody knew everybody else. "Maybe Leslie Coombes would help me."

"My God, Gus; don't let Ben hear you say that," Jack implored. "He'd blow up about a hundred megatons. You might just as well talk about getting V-dash-R G-dash-O to help."

"He could help a lot. If we ask him, he would."

"Ruth did a lot of work with juvenile court, on her cover-job," Ybarra mentioned. "There's some kind of a Juvenile Welfare Association . . ."

"Claudette Pendarvis. The Chief Justice's wife. She does a lot about Juvenile Welfare."

"Yes," Ybarra agreed instantly. "I've heard Ruth talk about her. Very favorably, too, and Ruth has a galloping allergy for volunteer do-gooders as a rule."

"She likes Fuzzies," Jack said. "She couldn't stay away from them during the trial. I promised her a pair as soon as I got a nice couple." He got to his feet. "Let's move into one of the offices, where we have a table to work on, and some communication screens. I'll call her now and ask her about it."

"Frederic, may I interrupt?"

Pendarvis turned from the reading-screen and started to lay aside his cigar and rise. Claudette, entering the room, motioned him to keep his seat and advanced to take the low cushion-stool, clasping her hands about her knees and tilting her head back in the same girlish pose he remembered from the long ago days on Baldur when he had been courting her.

"I want to tell you something lovely, Frederic," she

began. "Mr. Holloway just called me. He says he has two Fuzzies for me, a boy Fuzzy and a girl Fuzzy; he's going to have them brought in tomorrow or the next day."

"Well, that is lovely." Claudette was crazy about Fuzzies. Had been ever since the first telecasts of them, and she had watched them in court and visited them at the Hotel Mallory during the trial. Now that he considered, he would like a pair of Fuzzies, too. "I think I'll enjoy having them here as much as you will. I like Fuzzies, as long as they stay out of my courtroom."

They both laughed, remembering what seventeen Fuzzies and a Baby Fuzzy had done to the dignity of the court while their sapience was being debated.

"I hope this won't be regarded as special privilege though," he added. "A great many people want Fuzzies, and . . ."

"But other people can have Fuzzies, too. That was what Mr. Holloway was calling me about. They'll be made available for adoption, and he wants me to supervise it, to make sure they don't get into wrong hands and aren't mistreated."

That was something else. They'd both have to think about that carefully.

"You think it would be proper for you to have an official position like that?" he asked.

"I can't see why not. I'm doing the same kind of work with Juvenile Welfare."

"You'll be making decisions on who should and who should not be allowed to adopt Fuzzies. When I get a Native Cases Court set up — I think Yves Janiver, for that — your decisions will be accepted."

"Whose decisions do you think Adolphe Ruiz's Juvenile Court accepts now?"

"That's right," he agreed. And she couldn't accept the Fuzzies and refuse to help with the adoption bureau; that wouldn't be right, at all. And she wanted Fuzzies so badly. "Well, go ahead, darling; do it. Whoever takes that position will have to be somebody who really loves Fuzzies. What did you tell Mr. Holloway?"

"That I'd talk to you, and then call him back. He's at Government House now."

"Well, call him and tell him you accept. I'll call Yves and talk to him about the Native Cases Court..."

She had left the low seat while he was speaking; she stopped to kiss him on the way out. She'd be so happy. He hoped he wouldn't be too severely criticized. Well, he'd been criticized before and survived it.

Victor Grego watched Diamond investigating the articles on top of the low cocktail table. He took a couple of salted nuts from the glass bowl, nibbled one, and put the rest back. He looked at the half-full coffee cup and the liqueur glass, and left both alone. Then he started to pick up the ashtray.

"No, Diamond. *Vov*. Don't touch."

"*Vov ninta*, Diamond," Ernst Mallin, who was a slightly more advanced Fuzzy linguist, said. "We ought to learn their language, instead of making them learn ours."

"We ought to teach them our language, so they can speak to anybody, and not just Fuzzyologists."

"I deplore that term, Mr. Grego. The suffix is Greek, from *logos*. Fuzzy is not a Greek word, and should not be combined with it."

"Oh, rubbish, Ernst. We're not speaking Greek; we're speaking Lingua Terra. You know what Lingua Terra is? An indiscriminate mixture of English, Spanish, Portuguese and Afrikaans, mostly English. And you know what English is? The result of the efforts of Norman men-at-arms to make dates with Saxon barmaids in the Ninth Century Pre-Atomic, and no more legitimate than any of the other results. If a little Greek suffix gets into a mess like that, it'll have to take care of itself the best way it can. And you'd better learn to like the term, because it's your new title. Chief Fuzzyologist; fifteen percent salary increase."

Mallin gave one of his tight little smiles. "For that, I believe I can condone a linguistic barbarism."

Diamond seemed, he couldn't be sure, to be wanting to know why not touch; would it hurt?

"And how do you explain that he mustn't spill ashes on the floor, in his own language? What are the Fuzzy words for 'floor,' and 'ashes?' " He leaned forward and dropped the ash from his cigarette into the tray. "Ashtray," he said.

Diamond repeated it as well as he could. Then he strolled over to where Mallin sat. Mallin regarded smoking as an act of infantile oralism; his ashtray was empty.

"Asht'ay?" he asked. *"Diamond vov ninta?"*

"You see. He knows that ashtray is a class-word, not just the name of a specific object," Mallin said. "And I tried so hard to prove that Fuzzies couldn't generalize. This one is empty; let's see how we can explain the difference. If we give him the word 'ashes,' and then . . ."

A bell began ringing softly; Diamond turned quickly to see what it was. It was the bell for the private communication screen, and only half a dozen people knew the call-combination. He rose and put it on. Harry Steefer looked out of it.

"We found it, sir; ninth level down." That was the one below the first reported thefts and ransackings.

"The Fuzzies were penned in a small room that looks as though it had been intended for a general toilet and washroom. It's right off a main hall, and somebody's had an aircar in and out and set it down recently. I'd say half a dozen Fuzzies for two or three days."

"Good. I want to see it. I want Diamond to see it, too. Send somebody who knows where it is up to my private stage with a car small enough to get into it."

He blanked the screen and turned to Mallin. "You heard that. Well, let's all three of us go down and look at it." Jack Holloway stopped at the head of the long escalator and looked down into the garden, now double-lighted by Darius, almost full, and Xerxes, past full and just rising. After a moment he saw Ben Rainsford reclining in a lawn-chair, with Flora and Fauna snuggled together on his lap. As he started toward them, after descending, he thought they were all asleep. Then one of the Fuzzies stirred and yeeked, and Rainsford turned his head.

"Who is it?" he asked.

"Jack. Have you been here all evening?"

"Yes, all three of us," Rainsford said. "I think it's time for Fuzzies to go to bed, now."

"Ben, we just had a screen call from Company House. They found where those Fuzzies had been kept, an empty room on one of the unfinished floors. They showed us with a portable pickup; dark, filthy place. The Company police are working on it for physical evidence to corroborate Diamond's story. And they've put out a general want for those two Company rangers, Herckerd and Novaes; kidnapping and suspicion of enslavement."

"Who called you? Steefer?"

"Grego. He says we can count on him for anything. He's really sore about this."

The Fuzzies had jumped to the ground and were trying to attract his attention. Ben shifted in his chair, and began stuffing tobacco into his pipe.

"Jack." His voice was soft; he spoke hesitantly. "I've been talking to the kids, out here, till they got sleepy. They had a big time at Company House with Diamond. They say he's lonesome for other Fuzzies. They'd like him to come here and visit them, and they'd like to go back and visit him again."

"Well, a Fuzzy would get lonesome by himself. It didn't take Little Fuzzy long to go and bring the rest of his family into my place."

"And they say that outside that he's happy. They told me about all the nice things he had, and the garden, and the room that was fixed up for him. They say everybody's good to him, and Pappy Vic loves him. That's what they call Grego; Pappy Vic, just like they call us Pappy Ben and Pappy Jack." His lighter flared, showing a puzzled face above the pipe bowl. "I can't understand it, Jack. I thought Grego would hate Fuzzies."

"Why should he? The Fuzzies didn't know anything about the Company's charter; they don't know a Class-IV planet from Nifflheim. He doesn't even hate us; he'd have done the same thing in our place. Ben, he's willing to call the war off; why can't you?"

Rainsford puffed slowly, the smoke drifting and changing color in the double moonlight.

"Do you honestly believe that Fuzzy wants to stay with Grego?" he asked.

"It'd break Diamond's heart if you took him away from Pappy Vic. Ben, why don't you invite Diamond over to play with your two? You wouldn't have to meet

Grego; the girl he has helping with Diamond could bring him."

"Maybe I will. You're on speaking terms with Grego; why don't you?"

"I will, tomorrow." The Fuzzies hadn't wanted to play; they'd just wanted to be noticed. He picked Flora up and gave her to Ben, then took Fauna in his own arms. "Let's go put them to bed, and then go inside. We have a lot of things to do, in a hurry, and we need your authorization."

"Well, what?"

"Ahmed's staying here; he and Harry Steefer and Ian Ferguson and some others are having a conference tomorrow on this case and on general Fuzzy protection. And I'm setting up an Adoption Bureau; Judge Pendarvis' wife's agreed to take charge of that. We need laws, and till there's some kind of a legislature, you have to do that by decree."

"Well, all right. But there's one thing, Jack. Just because Grego's with us on this doesn't mean I'm going to let him grab back control of this planet, the way he had it before the Pendarvis Decisions. It took the Fuzzies to break the Company's monopoly; well, I'm going to see it stays broken."

X

KNOWING HENRY STENSON's part in the dischartering of the Zarathustra Company, Pancho Ybarra was mildly surprised to find him in the Fuzzy-room Grego had fitted up back of the kitchenette of his apartment, when Ernst Mallin, who met him on the landing stage, ushered him in. Grego's Fuzzy-sitter, Sandra Glenn, was there, and so, although in the middle of business hours, was Grego himself. And, of course, Diamond.

"Mr. Stenson," he greeted non-committally. "This is a pleasure."

Stenson laughed. "We needn't pretend to distant acquaintance, Lieutenant," he said. "Mr. Grego is quite aware of my, er, other profession. He doesn't hold it against me; he just insists that I no longer practice it on him."

"Mr. Stenson has something here that'll interest you," Grego said, picking up something that looked like a small nuclear-electric razor. "Turn off your hearing aid, if you please, Lieutenant. Thank you. Now, Diamond, make talk for Unka Panko."

"*Heyo, Unka Panko.*" Diamond said, when Grego held the thing to his mouth, very clearly and audibly.

101

"You hear Diamond make talk like Hagga?"

"I sure do, Diamond! That's wonderful."

"How make do?" Diamond asked. "Make talk with talk-thing, talk like Hagga. Not have talk-thing, no can talk like Fuzzy, Hagga no hear. How make do?"

Fuzzies could hear all through the human-audibility range; the race wouldn't have survived the dangers of the woods if they hadn't been able to. They could hear beyond that, to about 40,000 cycles. None of the other Zarathustran mammals could; that supported Gerd van Riebeek's theory that Fuzzies were living fossils, the sole survivors of a large and otherwise extinct order of Zara-thustran quasi-primates. Gerd thought they had de-veloped ultrasonic hearing to meet some ancient sur-vival-problem long before they had developed the power of symbolizing ideas in speech, and had always conversed ultrasonically with one another, probably to avoid be-traying themselves to their natural enemies.

"Fuzzies hear Big Ones talk. Fuzzies little, Hagga big, make big talk. Hagga not hear Fuzzy talk, Fuzzies little, make little talk. So, Big Ones make ear-things, make Fuzzy talk big in ears, can hear. Now, Hagga make talk-things, so Fuzzies make big talk like Hagga, everybody hear, have ear-things, not have ear-things."

That wasn't the question. Diamond had gotten that far, himself, already. The question, which he repeated, was, "How make do?"

Grego was grinning at him. "You're doing fine, Lieu-tenant. Now, go ahead and give him a lecture on ultra-sonics and electronics and acoustics."

"Has your Chief Fuzzyologist done anything on that yet?"

"I haven't even tried," Mallin said. "You know much more of the language than I do; what Fuzzy words would you use to explain anything like that?"

That was right. Any race — *Homo sapiens terra,* or *Fuzzy fuzzy holloway zarathustra* — thought just as far as their verbal symbolism went, and no further. And they could only comprehend ideas for which they had words.

"Just tell him it's Terran black magic," Sandra Glenn suggested.

That would work on planets like Loki or Thor or Yggdrasil; on Shesha or Uller, you could also mention the mysterious ways of the gods. The Fuzzies had just about as much conception of magic or religion as they had of electronics or nucleonics or the Abbot lift-and-drive.

He stooped forward and held out his hand. "*So-josso-aki,* Diamond. *So-pokko* Unka Panko."

The Fuzzy gave him the thing, which he had been holding in both hands. The resemblance to an electric razor was more than coincidental; the mechanism was enclosed in the plastic case of one. The end that would have done the shaving was open; the Fuzzy talked into that. There was a circular screened opening on the side from which the transformed sound emerged. It still had the original thumb-switch.

"Still has the original power-unit, too," Stenson said. That would be a little capsule the size of a 6-mm short pistol cartridge. "A lot of the parts are worked over from ultrasonic hearing-aid parts. I'm going to have to do something better than that switch, too. A little handle, maybe like a pistol grip, with a grip-squeeze switch, so that the Fuzzy will turn it on when he takes hold of it, and turn it off when he lets go. And it'll have to be a lot lighter and a lot smaller." He gestured toward some sheets of paper on which he had been making diagrams and schematics and notes. "I have some people at my shop working on that now. We'll have production prototypes in about a week. The Company's factory will start production as soon as they can tool up for it."

"We're getting a patent," Grego said. "We're calling it the Stenson Fuzzyphone."

"Grego-Stenson; it was your original idea."

"Hell, I just told you what I wanted; you invented it," Grego argued. "As soon as we have all the bugs chased out, we'll be in production. We don't know how much we'll have to ask for them. Not more than twenty sols, I don't suppose."

Flora and Fauna were puzzled. They sat on the floor at Pappy Ben's feet, looking up at the funny people that came and went in the picture-thing on the wall and spoke out of it. Long ago they had found out that nothing in the screen could get out of it, and they couldn't get in. It was just one of the strange things the Big Ones had, and they couldn't understand it, but it was fun.

But then, all of a sudden, there was Pappy Ben, right in the screen. They looked around, startled, thinking he had left them, but no, there he was, still in the chair smoking his pipe. They both felt him to make sure he was really there, then they both climbed onto his lap and pointed at the Pappy Ben in the screen.

Flora and Fauna didn't know about audiovisual recordings; they couldn't understand how Pappy Ben could be in two places at the same time. That bothered them. It just couldn't happen.

"It's all right, kids," he assured them. "I'm really here. That isn't me, there."

"Is," Flora contradicted. "I see it."

"Is not," Fauna told her. "Pappy Ben here."

Maybe Pancho Ybarra or Ruth van Riebeek could explain it; he couldn't.

"Of course I'm here," he said, hugging both of them. "That is just not-real look-like."

"It will be illegal," the Pappy Ben in the screen was saying, "to capture any Fuzzy in habitat by any other means, including the use of intoxicants, narcotics, sleep-gas, sono-stunners or traps. This will constitute kidnapping. It will be illegal to keep any Fuzzy chained, tied or otherwise physically restrained. It will be illegal to transport any Fuzzy from Beta Continent to any other part of this planet without a permit from the Native Affairs Commission, each permit to bear the fingerprints of the Fuzzy for whom it is issued. It will be illegal knowingly to deliver any Fuzzy to anybody intending to so transport him. This will constitute kidnapping, also, and will be punished accordingly."

The Pappy Ben in the screen was scowling menacingly. Flora and Fauna looked quickly around to see if the real Pappy Ben was mad about something too.

Flora said: "Make talk about Fuzzy."

"Yes. Talk about what Big Ones do to bad Big Ones who hurt Fuzzies," he told her.

"Make dead, like bad Big One who make Goldilocks dead?" Fauna asked.

"Something like that."

That was what all the Fuzzies who had been in court during the trial thought had happened. Suicide while of unsound mind due to remorse of conscience was a little too complicated to explain to a Fuzzy, at least at present.

All the Fuzzies who knew what had happened to Goldilocks thought that had been no more than the bad Big One deserved.

Captain Ahmed Khadra, chief of detectives, ZNPF, and Colonel Ian Ferguson, Commandant, Colonial Constabulary, were listening to the telecast with Max Fane, the Colonial Marshal, in the latter's office. In the screen, Governor Rainsford was saying:

"And any person capturing or illegally transporting or illegally holding in restraint any Fuzzy for purposes of sale will be guilty of enslavement."

"Aah!" Max Fane set a stiffly extended index finger against the base of his skull, cocked his thumb and clicked his tongue. "Death's mandatory; no discretion-of-the-court about it."

"Yves Janiver'll try all the Fuzzy cases. He likes Fuzzies," Ferguson said: "He won't like people who mistreat them."

"I know Janiver's attitude on death penalties," Fane said. "He doesn't think people should be shot for committing crimes; he thinks they should be shot for being the kind of people who commit them. He thinks shooting criminals is like shooting diseased veldbeest. A sanitation measure. So do I."

"If Herckerd and Novaes are smart, they'll come in and surrender now," Ferguson said. "You think they still have the other five?"

Khadra shook his head. "I think they sold them to somebody in Mallorysport as soon as they moved them out of Company House. If we could find out who that is . . ."

"I could name a dozen possibilities," Max Fane told him. "And back of each one of them is Hugo Ingermann."

"I wish we could haul Ingermann in and veridicate him," Ferguson said.

"Well, you can't. Ingermann's a lawyer, and the only

way you can question a lawyer under veridication is catch him standing over a corpse with a bloody knife in his hand. And you have a Nifflheim of a time doing it, even then."

"A great many people want Fuzzies; we know that," the Governor was saying. "Many of them should have them; they would make Fuzzies happy, and would be made happy by them. We are not going to deny such people an opportunity to adopt these charming little persons. An adoption bureau has been set up already; Mrs. Frederic Pendarvis, the wife of the Chief Justice, will be in charge of it, and the offices have already been set up in the Central Courts Building, and will open tomorrow morning..."

"Oh, Daddy; Mother!" the little girl cried. "You hear that, now. The Governor says people can have Fuzzies of their own. Won't you get me a Fuzzy? I'll be as good as good to it — him, I mean, or her, whichever."

The parents looked at one another, and then at their twelve-year-old daughter.

"What do you think, Bob?"

"You'll have to take care of it, Marjory, and that will be a lot of work. You'll have to feed it, and give it baths, and..."

"Oh, I will; I'll do anything, just if I can have one. And people mustn't call Fuzzies 'it,' Daddy; Fuzzies are people, too, like us. You didn't call me 'it,' when I was a little baby, did you?"

"I'm afraid your father did, my dear. Just at first. And you'll have to study and learn the language, so you can talk to the Fuzzy, because Fuzzies don't speak Lingua Terra. You know, Bob, I think I'd enjoy having a Fuzzy around, myself."

"You know, I believe I would, too. Well, let's get around to this adoption bureau the first thing tomorrow ..."

XI

THEY WERE having a party at the Pendarvis home. Jack Holloway sat on his heels on the floor, smoking his pipe and interpreting, while the judge and his wife, in a low easy-chair and on a drum-shaped hassock respectively, were getting acquainted with the guests of honor, the two Fuzzies Juan Jimenez had brought in from Beta Continent that evening. Gus Brannhard, who had come along from Government House, was sprawled in one of the larger chairs, chuckling in his beard. Juan Jimenez and Ahmed Khadra had removed their hearing-aids and carried their drinks to the other side of the room, where they were talking about Jimenez's visit, with a couple of George Lunt's troopers, to the site of his former camp.

"They were back, after we left," Jimenez was saying. "We could see where they'd set a car down. There wasn't much to see; they policed everything up very neatly after they left, the second time. Didn't leave any litter around."

"Or any evidence," Khadra added.

"That was what Yorimitsu and Calderon said when they saw it. I gather they take a dim view of neatness."

"Around where they're investigating, sure. Tidying up

around the scene of a crime's gotten more criminals off than all the crooked lawyers in the Galaxy. In this case it doesn't matter. Herckerd and Novaes brought those Fuzzies in; we know that. We have a witness."

"Can you veridicate a Fuzzy?" Brannhard asked, over his shoulder. "If you can't, the defense'll object."

Pendarvis looked up and around. "Mr. Brannhard, I'm afraid I'd have to sustain such an objection. I suspect that Judge Janiver, who'd be hearing the case, would, too. If I were you, I'd find out. Have you ever been veridicated?" he asked the Fuzzy on his lap.

The Fuzzy — the male member of the couple, who was trying to work the zipper of his jacket — said, "Unnh?" The judge scratched the back of his head, which the Fuzzy, like most furry people, liked, and wondered how long it would take to learn the language.

"Not too long," Jack told him. "It only took me a day to learn everything the people on Xerxes learned; by the time we were starting for home, after the trial, I could talk to them. What are you going to call them?"

"Don't they have names of their own, Mr. Holloway?" the judge's wife asked.

"They don't seem to. In the woods, there are never more than six or eight in a family, if that's what the groups are. I guess all the natives names are things like 'me,' and 'you,' and 'this one,' and 'that one.' "

"You'll have to have names for them, for the adoption papers," Brannhard said.

"At the camp, we just called them 'the Newlyweds,' " Khadra said.

"How about Pierrot and Columbine?" Mrs. Pendarvis asked.

Her husband nodded. "I think that would be fine." He pointed to himself. "*Aki Pappy Frederic. So Pierrot.*"

"Aki Py'hot? Py'hot siggo Pappy F'ed'ik."

"He accepts the name. He says he likes you. What are you going to do with them tomorrow, Mrs. Pendarvis? Do you have any human servants here?"

"No, everything's robotic, and I oughtn't to leave them alone with robots. Not till they get used to them."

"Drop them off at Government House; they can play with Flora and Fauna," Brannhard suggested. "And I'll call Victor Grego and invite his Diamond over, and they can have a real party. First Fuzzy social event of the season."

A mellow-toned bell began chiming. The Judge set Pierrot on the floor and excused himself; Pierrot trotted after him. In a moment, both were back.

"Chief Earlie's on screen," he said. "He wants to talk either to Captain Khadra or Mr. Holloway."

That was the new Mallorysport chief of police. Jack nodded to Khadra, who left the room.

"Probably found something out about Herckerd and Novaes," Brannhard said.

"Will you really charge them with enslavement?" Mrs. Pendarvis asked. "That's mandatory death."

"You catch people, deprive them of their freedom, make property of them," Brannhard said. "What else can you call it? A pet slave is still a slave, if he belongs to somebody else. I don't know how a Fuzzy could be made to work..."

"Nightclub entertainers, attractions in bars, sideshow acts..."

Khadra came back; he had his beret on, and was buckling on his pistol.

"Earlie says he has a report on a Fuzzy being seen in an apartment-unit over on the north side of the city," he said. "Informant says a Fuzzy is being kept by a

111

family on one of the upper floors. He's sending men there now."

That would probably be one of the five Herckerd and Novaes had brought in. He could see what had happened. The two former Company employees had sold them all to somebody here in Mallorysport, some racketeer who was selling them individually. There was somebody who really did need shooting. And by this time, Herckerd and Novaes would be back on Beta Continent, trapping more. Get the people who had bought this Fuzzy under veridication, the police had plenty of ways to make people want to talk, and work back from there.

"I'll go see what it is," Khadra was saying. "I'll call in as soon as I can. I don't know how long I'll be gone. In case I don't get back, thanks for a nice evening, Judge, Mrs. Pendarvis."

He hurried out, and for a moment nobody said anything. Then Jimenez suggested that if this were one of the Herckerd-Novaes lot, Diamond ought to see him as soon as possible; he'd be able to identify him. Khadra would think of that. Mrs. Pendarvis hoped there wouldn't be any shooting. Mallorysport city police were notoriously trigger-happy. The conversation continued by jerks and starts; the two Fuzzies seemed to be the only ones unconcerned.

After about an hour, Khadra returned; he had left his belt and beret in the hall.

"What was it?" Brannhard asked. Jack was wanting to know if the Fuzzy was all right.

"It wasn't a Fuzzy," Khadra said disgustedly. "It was a Terran marmoset; these people have had it for a couple of years; brought it from Terra. The people who own it have had a wire screen around their terrace to keep it, ever since they moved in. Somebody in an aircar saw it outside and thought it was a Fuzzy. I wonder how much more of this we're going to get."

It was a wonder he hadn't gotten that, himself, when his own family were lost and he was hunting for them.

XII

THE AIR traffic around Central Courts Building the next
morning seemed normal to Jack Holloway. There were
quite a few cars on the landing stage above the sixth
level down when he came in, but no more than he remembered from the time of the Fuzzy Trial. It was not
until he left the escalator on the fourth floor below,
where the Adoption Bureau officers were, that he began
to suspect that there was a Fuzzy rush on.

The corridor leading back from the main hall to the
suite that had been taken over yesterday was jammed.
It was a well behaved, well dressed, crowd, mostly couples clinging to each other to avoid being jostled apart.
Everybody seemed to be happy and excited; it was more
like a Year-End Holidays shopping crowd than anything
else.

A uniformed deputy-marshal saw him and approached,
touching his cap-brim in a half salute.

"Mr. Holloway; are you trying to get in to your
offices? You'd better come this way, sir; there's a queue
down at the other end."

There must be five or six hundred of them. Cut that
in half; most of them were couples.

"How long's this been going on?" he asked, noticing that several more couples and individuals were coming behind him.

"Since about 0700. There were a few here before then; the big rush didn't start till 0830."

Some of the people in the rear of the jam saw and recognized him. "Holloway." "Jack Holloway; he's the Commissioner." "Mr. Holloway; are there Fuzzies here now?"

The deputy took him down the hall and unlocked the door of an office; it was empty, and the desks and chairs and things shrouded in dust-covers. They went through and out into a back hall, where another deputy-marshal was arguing with some people who were trying to get in that way.

"Well, why are they letting him in; who's he?" a woman demanded.

"He works here. That's Jack Holloway."

"Oh! Mr. Holloway! Can you tell us how soon we can get Fuzzies?"

His guide rushed him, almost as though he were under arrest, along the hall, and opened another door.

"In here, Mr. Holloway; Mrs. Pendarvis' office. I'll have to get back and keep that mob in front straightened out." He touched his cap-brim again and hastened away.

Mrs. Pendarvis sat at a desk, her back to the door, going over a stack of forms in front of her. Beside her, at a smaller desk, a girl was taking them as she finished with them, and talking into the whisper-mouthpiece of a vocowriter. Two more girls sat at another desk, one talking to somebody in a communication screen. Mrs. Pendarvis said, "Who is it?" and turned her head, then rose, extending her hand. "Oh; Mr. Holloway. Good morning. What's it like out in the hall, now?"

"Well, you see how I had to come in. I'd say about five hundred, now. How are you handling them?"

She gestured toward the door to the front office, and he opened it and looked through. Five girls sat at five desks; each was interviewing applicants. Another girl was gathering up application-forms and carrying them to a desk where they were being sorted to be passed on to the back office.

"I arrived at 0830," Mrs. Pendarvis said. "Just after I dropped Pierrot and Columbine off at Government House. There was a crowd then, and it's been going on ever since. How many Fuzzies have you, Mr. Holloway?"

"Available for adoption? I don't know. Beside mine and Gerd and Ruth van Riebeek's and the Constabulary Fuzzies, there were forty day-before yesterday. That had gotten up to a hundred and three by last evening."

"We have, to date, three hundred and eleven applications; there are possible twenty more that haven't been sent back to me yet. By the time we close, it'll be five or six hundred. How are we going to handle this, anyhow? Some of these people want just one Fuzzy, some of them want two, some of them will take a whole family. And we can't separate Fuzzies who want to stay together. If you'd separate Pierrot and Columbine, they'd both grieve themselves to death. And there are families of five or six who want to stay together, aren't there?"

"Well, not permanently. These groups aren't really families; they're sort of temporary gangs for mutual assistance. Five or six are about as many as can make a living together in the woods. They're hunters and food-gatherers, low Paleolithic economy, and individual small-game hunters at that. When a gang gets too big to live together, they split up; when one couple meets another, they team up to hunt together. That's why they have such a well-developed and uniform language, and I imagine that's how the news about the zatku spread all over the Fuzzy country as fast as it did. They don't even mate permanently. Your pair are just young, first mating for both of them. They think each other are the most wonderful ever. But you will have others that won't want to be separated; you'll have to let them be adopted together." He thought for a moment. "You can't begin to furnish Fuzzies for everybody; why don't you give them out by lot? Each of those applications is numbered, isn't it? Draw numbers."

"Like a jury-drawing, of course. Let the jury-commissioners handle that," the Chief Justice's wife said.

"Fair enough. You'll have to investigate each of these applicants, of course; that'll take a little time, won't it?"

"Well, Captain Khadra's taking charge of them. He's borrowed some people from the schools, and some from the city police juvenile squad and some from the Company personnel division. I've been getting my staff together the same way — parent-teacher groups, Juvenile Welfare. I'm going to get a paid staff together, as soon as I can. I think they'll come from the Company's public-service division; I'm told that Mr. Grego's going to suspend all those activities in ninety days."

"That's right. That includes the schools, and the hospitals. Why don't you talk to Ernst Mallin? He'll find you all the people you want. He's joined the Friends of Little Fuzzy, too, now."

"Well, after we've allocated Fuzzies to these people, what then? Do they come out to your camp and pick their own?"

"Good Lord, no! We have enough trouble, without having the place overrun with human people." He hadn't given that thought until now. "What we'll need will be a place here in Mallorysport where a couple of hundred Fuzzies can stay and where the people who have been endorsed for foster-parents can come and select the ones they want."

That would have to be a big place, with a park all around it, that could be fenced in to keep them from wandering off and getting lost. A nice place, where they could all have fun together. He didn't know of any such place, and asked her about it.

"I'll talk to Mr. Urswick, he's the Company Chief of Public Services. He'll know about something. You know, Mr. Holloway, I didn't have any idea, when I took this job, that it was going to be so complicated."

"Mrs. Pendarvis, I've been saying that every hour on the hour since I let Ben Rainsford talk me into taking the job I have. You're going to have to do something about information, too — Fuzzies, care and feeding of; Fuzzies, psychology of; language. We'll try to find somebody to prepare booklets and language-learning tapes. And hearing-aids."

The door at the side of the room was marked INVESTIGATION. He found Ahmed Khadra in the room behind it, talking to somebody in a city police uniform by screen.

"Well, have you gotten anything from any of them?" he was asking.

"Damn little," the city policeman told him. "We've been pulling them in all day, everybody in town who has a record. And Hugo Ingermann's been pulling them away from us as fast as they come in. He had a couple of his legmen and assistants here with portable radios, and as fast as we bring some punk in, they call somebody at Central Courts and he gets a writ; order to show grounds for suspicion. Most of them we can't question at all; it takes an hour to an hour and a half from the time they're brought in before we can veridicate those we can. And none of them knows a damn thing when we do."

"Well, how about known associates? Didn't either of them have any friends?"

"Yes. All middle-salary Company people; they've been cooperating, but none of them know anything."

The conversation went on for a few more minutes, then they blanked screens. Khadra turned in his chair and lit a cigarette.

"Well, you heard it, Jack," he said. "They just vanished, and the Fuzzies with them. I'm not surprised we're not getting anything out of their friends in the Company. They wouldn't know. We searched their rooms; they seem to have cleaned out everything they had when they disappeared. And we can't get anything from underworld sources. None of the city police stool-pigeons know anything."

"You know, Ahmed, I'm worried about that. I wonder what's happened to those Fuzzies . . ." He sat down on the edge of the desk and got out his pipe and tobacco. "How soon will you be able to start investigating these people who want Fuzzies?"

Gerd van Riebeek refilled his cup and shoved the coffee across the table to George Lunt. He ought to be getting back to work; they both ought to. Work was piling up, with both Jack and Pancho away and Ahmed Khadra permanently detached from duty at the camp.

"Eighty-seven," Lunt said. "That's not counting yours and mine and Jack's."

"The Extee Three's getting low." They'd had to start rationing it; tomorrow, they'd not be able to issue any, or on alternate days thereafter. The Fuzzies wouldn't like that. "Jacks says he thinks speculators are buying it and holding it off the market. They'll get big prices for it when the Fuzzies start coming in to Mallorysport."

There wasn't much Extee Three on Zarathustra. People kept a tin or so in their aircars, in case of forced landings in the wilderness which was ninety percent of the planet's land surface, but until the Fuzzies found out about it, the consumption had been practically zero. There was a supply on Xerxes, for emergency ships' stores, individual survival kits and so on, but that wouldn't last. It was on order, but it would be four months till any could get in from the nearest Federation planet. And the supply on hand wouldn't last that long.

"Personally, I wish there was eighty-seven hundred of them," Lunt said. "No, I'm not crazy, and I mean it. The ones we have here aren't getting into deviltry down in the farming country. So far, I haven't heard of any of them getting that far, except that one family that's moved in on that backwoods farm, and they're behaving themselves. But wait till they get down in the real farm-country, and among the sugar plantations. You know, Jack and I thought, at first, that our big job was going to be protecting Fuzzies from humans. It looks to me, now, like it's going to be the other way round too."

"That's right. They won't mean any harm; the only malicious thing I ever heard of Fuzzies doing was the time Jack's family wrecked Juan Jimenez's office, after they broke out of the cages he put them in, and I don't blame them for that. But they just don't understand about what they mustn't do among humans. They don't seem to have any idea at all of property in the absence of a visible owner."

"That's what I'm talking about. Crops; they won't understand that somebody's planted them, they'll think they're just there. And I never saw a farmer that wouldn't shoot first and argue afterward to protect his crops."

"Education," Gerd said.

"Recipe for roast turkey—first catch a turkey," Lunt said. "We're educating this crowd. How in Nifflheim are we going to catch all the other ones?"

"Educate the farmers. What do Fuzzies eat, beside Extee Three?"

"Zatku, and they've cleaned all of them out around the camp. That's why we have to have one car patroling a couple of miles out to shoot harpies off."

"And do you know any kind of crops land-prawns don't destroy? I was making a study of them, for a while. I don't. That's what I mean by educating the farmers. A Fuzzy does X-much damage to crops. He kills half a dozen land-prawns a day, and among them they do about X-times-ten damage."

"Write up a script about it, and we'll put it on the air this evening. 'Be good to Fuzzies; Fuzzies are the farmer's best friend.' Maybe that'll help some."

Gerd nodded. "Eighty-seven, we have now. How many little ones?"

"Beside Baby Fuzzy? Four. Why?"

"And we think we have five pregnancies. That's all Lynne Andrews is sure of; the only way she can tell is listening with a stethoscope for fetal movements. They seem to be too small to make any conspicuous visible difference. This is out of eighty seven. What kind of a birthrate do you call that, George?"

George Lunt poured more coffee into his cup and blew on it automatically. Somewhere, maybe Constabulary

School, the coffee had always been too hot to drink right away. Across the messhall, half a dozen Fuzzies tagged behind a robot, watching it clear the tables.

"It sure to Nifflheim isn't any population explosion," he said.

"Race extinction, George. I don't know what the normal life expectancy is in the woods, but I'd say four out of five of them die by violence. When the birthrate curve drops below the deathrate curve, a race is dying out."

"A hundred and two Fuzzies, and four children. Hey, you said five of the girls were pregnant, didn't you? And you admit that's not complete, if Doc Andrews has to use a stethoscope for a pregnancy-test."

"I wondered if you'd notice that. That's not a bad ratio, for females who have a monthly cycle instead of an annual mating season. And these four children; we don't know anything about the maturation period, but in the three months we've been checking on him, Baby Fuzzy's only gained six ounces and an inch. I'd make it about fifteen years, ten at very least."

"Then," Lunt said, "it isn't birthrate at all. It's infant mortality. They just don't live."

"That's it, George. That's what I'm worried about. And Ruth and Lynne, too. If we don't find out what causes it, and how to stop it, there won't be any Fuzzies after a while."

"This is like old times, Victor," Coombes said, stretching in one of the chairs. "Nobody here but us humans."

"That's right." He brought the jug and the two glasses over and put them on the low table, careful not to disturb a pattern of colored tiles laid on one end of it. "That thing there is a Fuzzy work of art. It is unfinished, but just see the deep symbolic significance."

"You see it. I can't." Coombes accepted his glass with mechanical thanks and sipped. "Where is everybody?"

"Diamond is a guest, at a place where I'm not welcome. Government House. He and Flora and Fauna are meeting Pierrot and Columbine, Judge and Mrs. Pendarvis' Fuzzies. Sandra is chaperoning the affair, and Ernst is conferring with Mrs. Pendarvis about quarters for a couple of hundred Fuzzies who are coming to town in about a week to be adopted."

"I'll say this: your Fuzzy and Fuzzyologists are getting in with the right people. Did you hear Hugo Ingermann's telecast this afternoon?"

"I did not. I pay people to do that kind of work for me. I went over a semantically correct summary, with a symbolic-logic study. As nearly as I can interpret it, it reduces to the propositions that, A) Ben Rainsford is a bigger crook than Victor Grego, and, B) Victor Grego is a bigger crook than Ben Rainsford, and, C) between them, they are conspiring to rob and enslave everybody on the planet, Fuzzies included."

"I listened to it very carefully, and recorded it, in the hope that he might forget himself and say something actionable. He didn't; he's lawyer enough to know what's libel and what isn't. Sometimes I dream of being able to sue that bastard for something, so that I can get him in the stand under veridication, but . . ." He shrugged.

"I noticed one thing. He's attacking the Company, and he's attacking Rainsford, but at the same time he's trying to drive wedges between us, so we won't gang up on him."

"Yes. That spaceport proposition. 'Why doesn't our honest and upright Governor do something to end this infamous space-transport monopoly of the Company's, which is strangling the economy of the planet?' "

"Well, why doesn't he? Because it would cost about fifty million sols, and ships using it would have to load and unload from orbit. But that sounds like a real live issue to the people who don't think and have nothing to think with, which means a large majority of the voters. You know what I'm worried about, Leslie? Ingermann attacking Rainsford for collusion with the Company. He hammers at that point long enough, and Rainsford's going to do something to prove he isn't, and whatever it is, it'll hurt us."

"That's the way it looks to me, too," Coombes agreed. "You know, among the many benefits of the Pendarvis Decisions, we now have a democratic government on Zarathustra. That means, we now have politics here. Ingermann controls all the other rackets, and politics is the biggest racket there is. Hugo Ingermann is running himself for political boss of Zarathustra."

XIII

The aircar settled to the ground; the Marine sergeant at the controls, who had been expecting to smash a dozen or so Fuzzies getting down, gave a whoosh of relief. Pancho Ybarra opened the door and motioned his companion, in Marine field-greens, to precede him, then stepped to the ground. George Lunt, still in his slightly altered Constabulary uniform, and Gerd van Riebeek, in bush-jacket and field-boots, advanced to meet them, accompanied by a swarm of Fuzzies. They all greeted him enthusiastically, and then wanted to know where Pappy Jack was.

"Pappy Jack in Big House Place; not come this place with Unka Panko. Pappy Jack come this place soon; two lights-and-darks," he told them. "Pappy Jack have to make much talk with other Big Ones."

"Make talk about Fuzzies?" Little Fuzzy wanted to know. "Find Big Ones for all Fuzzies?"

"That's right. Find place for Fuzzies to go in Big House Place," he said.

"He's been on that ever since Jack went away," Gerd said. "All the Fuzzies are going to have Big Ones of their own, now."

"Well, Jack's working on it," he said. "You've both met Captain Casagra, haven't you? Gerd van Riebeek; Major Lunt. The captain's staying with us a couple of days; tomorrow Lieutenant Paine and some reinforcements are coming out; fifty men and fifteen combat-cars, to help out with the patroling till we can get men and vehicles of our own."

"Well, I'm glad to hear that, Captain!" Lunt said. "We're very short of both."

"You have a lot of country to patrol, too," Casagra said. "As Navy-Lieutenant Ybarra says, I'll only stay a few days, to get the feel of the situation. Marine-Lieutenant Paine will stay till you can get your own force recruited up and trained. That is, if things don't blow up again in the veldbeest country."

"Well, I hope they don't," Lunt said. "The vehicles are as welcome as the men; we have very few of our own."

"The Company's making some available," he said. "And along with his other work, Ahmed Khadra's starting a ZNPF recruiting drive."

"Has Jack been able to get his hands on any more Extee Three?" Gerd wanted to know.

He shook his head. "He hasn't even been able to get any for the reception center, when the Fuzzies start coming in to town. The Company's going to start producing it, but that'll take time. After they get the plant set up, they'll probably be running off test batches for a couple of weeks before they get one right."

"The formula's very simple," Casagra said.

"Some of the processes aren't; I was talking to Victor Grego. His synthetics people aren't optimistic, but Grego's whip-cracking at them to get it done yesterday morning."

"Isn't that something?" Gerd asked. "Victor Grego, Fuzzy-lover. And Jimenez, and Mallin; you ought to have heard the language my refined and delicate wife used when she heard about that."

"Last war's enemies, next war's allies," Casagra laughed. "I spent a couple of years on Thor; clans that'd be shooting us on sight one season would be our bosom friends the next, and planning to double-cross us the one after."

An aircar rose from behind the ZNPF barracks across the run and started south; another, which had been circling the camp five miles out, was coming in.

"Happy patrol," Lunt was explaining to Casagra. "The Fuzzies cleaned out all the zatku, land-prawns, around the camp, and they've been hunting farther out each day. Harpies like Fuzzies the way Fuzzies like zatku, so we have to give them air-cover. That's been since you left, Pancho; we've shot about twenty harpies since then. Four up to noon today; I don't know how many since."

"Lost any Fuzzies yet?"

"Not to harpies, no. We almost had a lot of them massacred yesterday; two of these families or whatever they are got into a *shoppo-diggo* fight about some playthings. A couple got chopped up a little; there's one." He pointed to a Fuzzy with a white bandage turbaned about his head; he seemed quite proud of it. "One got a broken leg; Doc Andrews has him in the hospital with his leg in a cast. Before I could get to the fight, Little Fuzzy and Ko-Ko and Mamma Fuzzy and a couple of my crowd had broken it up; just waded in with their flats as if they'd been doing riot-work all their lives. And you ought to have heard Little Fuzzy chewing them out afterward. Talked to them like an old sergeant in boot-camp."

"Oh, they fight among themselves?" Casagra asked.

"This is the first time it's happened here. I suppose they do, now and then, in the woods, with their wooden *zatku-hodda*. They have a regular fencing system. Nothing up to Interstellar Olympic epée standards, but effective. That's why half of them weren't killed in the first five seconds." Lunt looked at his watch. "Well, Captain, suppose you come with me; we'll go to Protection Force headquarters and go over what we've been doing and how your Lieutenant Paine and his men can help out."

Casagra went over to the car and spoke to the sergeant at the controls, then he and Lunt climbed in. Ybarra fell in with Gerd and they started in the direction of the lab-hut.

"One of the pregnancy cases lost her baby," Gerd said. "It was born prematurely and dead. We have the baby, fetus rather, under refrigeration. It seems to be about equivalent to human six-month stage. It wouldn't have survived in any case. Malformed, visibly and I suppose internally as well. We haven't done anything with it, yet; Lynne wanted you to see it. The Fuzzies were all sore; they thought it rated a funeral. We managed to explain to Little Fuzzy and a couple of others what we wanted to do with it, and they tried to explain to the others. I don't know how far any of it got."

The Fuzzies with them ran ahead, shouting *"Mummy Woof! Auntie Lynne! Unka Panko bizzo do-mitto!"* They were all making a clamor inside the lab-hut when he and Gerd entered, and Ruth, who was working at one of the benches making some kind of a test, was trying to shush them.

"Heyo, Unka Panko," she greeted him, hastening

through with what she had at hand. "I'll be loose in a jiffy." She made a few notes, set a test-tube in a rack and made a grease-pencil number on it, and then pulled down the cover and locked it. "I haven't done this since med-school. Lynne's back in the dispensary with a couple of volunteer native nurses, looking after the combat-casualty." She got cigarettes out of her smock-pocket and lit one, then dropped into a chair. "Pancho, what *is* this about Ernst Mallin?" she asked. "Do you believe it?"

"Yes. He's really interested, now that he doesn't have to prove any predetermined Company-policy points about them. And he really like Fuzzies. I've seen him with that one of Grego's, and with Ben's Flora and Fauna, and Mrs. Pendarvis' pair."

"I wouldn't believe it, even if I saw it. I saw what he did to Id and Superego and Complex and Syndrome. It's a wonder all four of them aren't incurably psychotic."

"But they aren't; they're just as sane as any other Fuzzies. Mallin's sorry for doing what he did with them, but he isn't sorry about what he learned from them. He says Fuzzies are the only people he's ever seen who are absolutely sane and can't be driven out of sanity. He says if humans could learn to think like Fuzzies, it would empty all the mental hospitals and throw all the psychiatrists out of work."

"But they're just like little children. Dear, smart little children, but . . ."

"Maybe children who are too smart to grow up. Maybe we'd be like Fuzzies, too, if we didn't have a lot of adults around us from the moment we were born, infecting us with non-sanity. I hope we don't begin infecting the Fuzzies, now. What was this fight all about, the other day?"

"Well, it was about some playthings, over in the big

Fuzzy-shelter. This new crowd that came in that day saw them and wanted to take them. They were things that were intended for everybody to play with, but they didn't know that. There was an argument, and the next thing the *shoppo-diggo* were going. The crowd who started it are all sorry, now, and everybody's friends."

Lynne came through the door from the dispensary at the end of the hut. A couple of Fuzzies were running along with her. Some of the Fuzzies who had come in from outside with them drifted in through the dispensary door, to visit their wounded friend. Lynne came over and joined them. Gerd asked about the patient; the patient was doing well, and being very good about staying in bed.

"How about the girl who lost her baby?" he asked.

"She's running around as though nothing had happened. It was heartbreaking, Pancho. The thing—it was so malformed that I'm not sure it was male or female —was born dead. She looked at it, and touched it, and then she looked up at me and said, '*Hudda. Shi-nozza.*'"

"Dead. Like always," Gerd said. "She acted as though it were only what she'd expected. I don't think more than ten percent of them live more than a few days. You want to see it, Pancho?"

He didn't, particularly; it wasn't his field. But then, Fuzzy embryology wasn't anybody's field, yet. They went over to one of the refrigerators, and Gerd got it out and unwrapped it. It was smaller than a mouse, and he had to use a magnifier to look at it. The arms and legs were short and under-developed; the head was malformed, too.

"I can't say anything about it," he said, "except that it's a good thing it was born dead. What are you going to do with it?"

"I don't want to dissect it myself," Lynne said. "I'm not competent. That's too important to bungle with."

"I'm no good at dissection. Take it in to Mallorysport Hospital; that's what I'd do." He re-wrapped the tiny thing and put it back. "The more of you work in it, the less you'll miss. You want to find everything out you can."

"That's what I'm going to do. I'll call them now, and see who all can help, and when."

Half a dozen Fuzzies came in from outside; they were carrying a dead land-prawn. Some of the Fuzzies already in the hut ran ahead of them, into the dispensary.

"Come on, Pancho; let's watch," Gerd said. "They're bringing a present for their sick friend. They must have dragged that thing three or four miles."

There were five Fuzzies and two other people in the west lower garden of Government House, as the aircar came in. The other people were Captain Ahmed Khadra, ZNPF, and Sandra Glenn, so the five Fuzzies would be the host and hostess, Fauna and Flora, and Pierrot and Columbine Pendarvis and Diamond Grego. They had a red and gold ball, two feet, or one Fuzzy-height, in diameter, and they were pushing and chasing it about the lawn. Every once in a while, they would push it to where Khadra was standing, and then he would give it a kick and send it bounding. Jack Holloway chuckled; it looked like the kind of romping he and his Fuzzies had done on the lawn beside his camp, when there had been a lawn there and when there had just been his own Fuzzies.

"Ben, drop me down there, will you?" he said. "I feel like a good Fuzzy-romp, right now."

"So do I," Rainsford said. "Will, set us down, if you please."

The pilot circled downward, holding the car a few inches above the grass while they climbed out. The Fuzzies had seen the car descend and came pelting over. At first, he thought they were carrying pistols; at least, they wore belts and small holsters. The things in the holsters had pistol-grips, but when they drew them, he saw that they were three-inch black discs, which the Fuzzies held to their mouths.

"Pappy Ben; Pappy Jack!" they were all yelling. "Listen; we talk like Big Ones, now!"

He snapped off his hearing-aid. It was true; they were all speaking audibly.

"Pappy Vic make," Diamond said proudly.

"Actually, Henry Stenson made them," the girl said. "At least, he invented them. All Mr. Grego did was tell him what he wanted. They are Fuzzyphones."

"*Heeta,* Pappy Jack." Diamond held his up. "Yeek-yeek. *Yeeek!*" He was exasperated, and then remembered he'd taken it away from his mouth. "Fuzzy-talk go in here, this side. Inside, grow big. Come out this side, big like Hagga-talk," he said, holding the device to his mouth.

"That good, Diamond. Good-good," he commended. "What do you think of this, Ben?"

Rainsford squatted in front of his own Fuzzies, holding out a hand. "*So-pokko-aki,* Flora," he said, and the Fuzzy handed him hers, first saying, "*Keffu,* Pappy Ben; *do' brek.*"

"I won't." Rainsford looked at it curiously, and handed it back. "That thing's good. Little switch on the grip, and it looks as though the frequency-transformer's in the middle and they can talk into either side of it."

It would have to work that way; Fuzzies were ambidextrous. Gerd had a theory about that. Fuzzies weren't anatomists, mainly because they didn't produce fire and didn't cut up the small animals they killed for cooking, and only races who had learned the location and importance of the heart fought with their hearts turned away from the enemy. *Homo sapiens terra's* ancestors in the same culture-stage were probably ambidextrous too. Like most of Gerd's theories, it made sense.

"Who makes these things?" he asked. "Stenson?"

"He made these, in his shop. The CZC electronics equipment plant is going to manufacture them," the girl said, adding: "Advertisement."

"You tell Mr. Grego to tell his electronics plant to get cracking on them. The Native Affairs Commission wants a lot of them."

"You staying for dinner with us, Miss Glenn?" Rainsford asked.

"Thank you, Governor, but I have to take Diamond home."

"I have to take Pierrot and Columbine home, too," Khadra said. "What are you doing this evening?"

"I have my homework to do. Fuzzy language lessons."

"Well, why can't I help you with your homework?" Khadra wanted to know. "I speak Fuzzy like a native, myself."

"Well, if it won't be too much trouble . . ." she began.

Holloway laughed. "Who are you trying to kid, Miss Glenn? Look in the mirror if you think teaching you Fuzzy would be too much trouble for anybody Ahmed's age. If I was about ten years younger, I'd pull rank on him and leave him with the Fuzzies."

Pierrot and Columbine thought all this conversation boring and irrelevant. They trundled the ball over in front of Khadra and commanded: *"Mek kikko!"*

Khadra kicked the ball, lifting it from the ground and sending it soaring away. The Fuzzies ran after it.

"Dr. Mallin says you were looking at the sanatorium," Sandra said.

"Yes. That's going to be a good place. You know about it?" he asked Khadra.

"Well, it's a big place," Khadra said. "I've seen it from the air, of course. They only use about ten percent of it, now."

"Yes. We're taking a building, intended for a mental ward; about a half square mile of park around it, with a good fence, so the Fuzzies won't stray off and get lost. We could put five-six hundred Fuzzies in there, and they wouldn't be crowded a bit. And it'll be some time before we get that many there at one time. I expect there'll be about a hundred to a hundred and fifty this time next week."

"There were precisely eight hundred and seventy-two applications in when the office closed this evening," Khadra said. "When are you going back, Jack?"

"Day after tomorrow. I want to make sure the work's started on the reception center, and I'm still trying to locate some Extee-Three. I think a bunch of damn speculators have cornered the market and are holding it for high prices."

The Fuzzies had pushed the ball into some shrubbery and were having trouble dislodging it. Sandra Glenn started off to help them, Ben Rainsford walking along with her. Khadra said:

"That'll probably be some of Hugo Ingermann's crowd, too."

"Speaking about Ingermann; how are you making out about Herckerd and Novaes?" he asked. "And the five Fuzzies."

"Jack, I swear. I'm beginning to think Herckerd and Novaes and those Fuzzies all walked into a mass-energy converter together. That's how completely all of them have vanished."

"They hadn't sold them before Ben's telecast, evening before last. After that, with the Adoption Bureau opening all that talk about kidnapping and enslavement and so on, nobody would buy a bootleg Fuzzy. So they couldn't sell them, so they got rid of them." How? That was what bothered him. If they'd used sense, they'd have flown them back to Beta and turned them loose. He was afraid, though, that they'd killed them. By this time everybody knew that live Fuzzies could tell tales. "I think those Fuzzies are dead."

"I don't know. Eight hundred and seventy-two applications, and a hundred and fifty Fuzzies at most," Khadra said. "There'll be a market for bootleg Fuzzies. Jack, you know what I think? I think those Fuzzies weren't brought in for sale. I think this gang—Herckerd and Novaes and whoever else is in with them—are training those Fuzzies to help catch other Fuzzies. Do you think a Fuzzy could be trained to do that?"

"Sure. To all intents and purposes, that's what our Fuzzies are doing out at the camp. You know how Fuzzies think? Big Ones are a Good Thing. Any Fuzzy who has a Big One doesn't need to worry about anything. All Fuzzies ought to have Big Ones. That's what Little Fuzzy has been telling the ones from the woods, out at camp. Ahmed, I think you have something."

"I thought of something else, too. If this gang can make a deal with some tramp freighter captain, they could ship Fuzzies off-planet and make terrific profits on it. You wait till the news about the Fuzzies gets around. There'll be a sale for them everywhere—Terra,

Odin, Freya, Marduk, Aton, Baldur, planets like that. Anybody can bring a ship into orbit on this planet, now, if he has his own landing-craft and doesn't use the CZC spaceport. In a month, word will have gotten to Gimli, that's the nearest planet, and in two more months a ship can get here from there."

"Spaceport. That could be why Ingermann's been harping on this nefarious CZC space-terminal monopoly. If he had a little spaceport of his own, now . . ."

"Any kind of smuggling you can think of," Khadra said. "Hot sunstones. Narcotics. Or Fuzzies."

Rainsford and Sandra Glenn were approaching; Sandra carried Diamond, Pierrot and Columbine ran beside her, and Flora and Fauna were trundling the ball ahead of them. He wanted to talk to Rainsford about this. They needed more laws, to prohibit shipping Fuzzies off-planet; nobody'd thought of that possibility before. And talk to Grego; the company controlled the only existing egress from the planet.

Lynne Andrews straightened and removed the binocular loop and laid it down, blinking. The others, four men and two women in lab-smocks, were pushing aside the spotlights and magnifiers and cameras on their swinging arms and laying down instruments.

"That thing wouldn't have lived thirty seconds, even if it hadn't been premature," one man said. "And it doesn't add a thing to what we don't know about Fuzzy embryology." He was an embryologist, human-type, himself. "I have dissected over five hundred aborted fetuses and I never saw one in worse shape than that."

"It was so tiny," one of the women said. She was an obstetrician. "I can't believe that that's human six-months equivalent."

"Well, I can," somebody else said. "I know what a young Fuzzy looks like; I spent a lot of time with Jack Holloway's Baby Fuzzy, during the trial. And I don't suppose a fertilized Fuzzy ovum is much different from one of ours. Between the two, there has to be a regular progressive development. I say this one is two-thirds developed. Misdeveloped, I should say."

"Misdeveloped is correct, Doctor. Have you any idea why this one misdeveloped as it did?"

"No, Doctor, I haven't."

"They come from northern Beta; that country's never been more than air-scouted. Does anybody know what radioactivity conditions are, up there? I've seen pictures of worse things than this from nuclear bomb radiations on Terra during and after the Third and Fourth World Wars, at the beginning of the First Federation."

"The country hasn't been explored, but it's been scanned. Any natural radioactivity strong enough to do that would be detectable from Xerxes."

"Oh, Nifflheim; that fetus could have been conceived on a patch of pitchblende no bigger than this table . . ."

"Well, couldn't it be chemical? Something in the pregnant female's diet?" the other woman asked.

"The Thaladomide Babies!" somebody exclaimed. "First Century, between the Second and Third World Wars. That was due to chemicals taken orally by pregnant women."

"All right; let's get the biochemists in on this, then."

"Chris Hoenveld," somebody else said. "It's not too late to call him now."

Fuzzies didn't have Cocktail Hour; that was for the Big Ones, to sit together and make Big One talk. Fuzzies just came stringing in before dinner, more or less interested in food depending on how the hunting had been, and after they ate they romped and played until they were tired, and then sat in groups, talking idly until they became sleepy.

In the woods, it had not been like that. When the sun began to go to bed, they had found safe places, where the big animals couldn't get at them, and they had snuggled together and slept, one staying awake all the time. But here the Big Ones kept the animals away, and killed them with thunder-things when they came too close, and it was safe. And the Big Ones had things that made light even when the sky was dark, and there were places where it was always bright as day. So here, there was more fun, because there was less danger, and many new things to talk about. This was the *Hoksu-Mitto,* the Wonderful Place.

And today, they were even happier, because today Pappy Jack had come back.

Little Fuzzy got out his pipe, the new one Pappy Jack had brought from the Big House Place, and stuffed it with tobacco, and got out the little fire-maker. Some of the Fuzzies around him, who had just come in from the woods, were frightened. They were not used to fire; when fire happened in the woods, it was bad. That was wild fire, though. The Big Ones had tamed fire, and if a person were careful not to touch it or let it get loose, fire was nothing to be afraid of.

"We go other places, and all have Big Ones, tomorrow?" one asked. "Big Ones for us, like Pappy Jack for you?"

"Not tomorrow. Not next day. Day after that." He held up three fingers. "Then go in high-up-thing, to place like this. Big Ones come, make talk. You like Big

One, Big One like you, you go with Big One, you live in Big One place."

"Nice place, like this?"

"Nice place. Not like this. Different place."

"Not want to go. Nice place here, much fun."

"Then you not go. Pappy Jack not make you go. You want to go, Pappy Jack find nice Big One for you, be good to you."

"Suppose not good. Suppose bad to us?"

"Then Pappy Jack come, Pappy Jorj, Unka Ahmed, Pappy Ge'hd, Unka Panko; make much trouble for bad Big One, *bang, bang, bang!*"

XIV

Myra was vexed. "It's Mr. Dunbar. The chief chemist at Synthetic Foods," she added, as though he didn't know that. "He is here himself; he has something he insists he must give to you personally."

"That's what I told him to do, Myra. Send him in."

Malcolm Dunbar pushed through the door from Myra's office with an open fiberboard carton under his arm. That had probably helped vex Myra; Dunbar was an executive, and executives ought not to carry their own parcels; it was *infra dignitatem*. He set it on the corner of the desk.

"Here it is, Mr. Grego; this is the first batch. We just finished the chemical tests on it. Identical with both the Navy stuff and the stuff we imported ourselves."

He rose and went around the desk, reaching into the carton and taking out a light brown slab, breaking off a corner and tasting it. It had the same slightly rancid, slightly oily and slightly sweetish flavor as the regular product. It tasted as though it had been compounded according to the best scientific principles of dietetics, by somebody who thought there was something sinful about eating for pleasure. He yielded to no one in his admiration of *Fuzzy fuzzy holloway,* but anybody who liked this stuff was nuts.

"You're sure it's safe?"

Dunbar was outraged. "My God, would I bring it here for you to feed your Fuzzy if I didn't know it was? In the first place, it's made strictly according to Terran Federation Armed Forces specifications. The bulk-matter is pure wheat farina, the same as Argentine Syntho-Foods and Odin Dietetics use. The rest is chemically pure synthetic nutrients. We have a man at the plant who used to be a chemical engineer at Odin Dietetics; he checked all the processes and they're identical. And we tried it on all the standard lab-animals; Terran hamsters and Thoran tilbras, and then on Freyan kholphs and Terran rhesus monkeys. The kholphs," he footnoted, "didn't like it worth a damn. It harmed none of them. And I ate a cake of the damned stuff myself, and it took a couple of hours and a pint of bourbon to get rid of the taste," the martyr to science added.

"All right. I will accept that it is fit for Fuzzy consumption. Fortunately, the whole Fuzzy population of Mallorysport, all five of them, are up on my terrace now. Let's go."

Ben Rainsford's Flora and Fauna, and Mrs. Pendarvis' Pierrot and Columbine were with Diamond in the Fuzzy-room. Outside on the terrace it was raw and rainy, one of Mallorysport's rare unpleasant days. They had a lot of colored triangular tiles on the floor, and were making patterns with them. Sandra Glenn was watching them with one eye and reading with the other. They all sprang to their feet and began yeeking, then remembered the Fuzzy phones on their belts, whipped them out, and began shouting, *"Heyo, Pappy Vic!"* He'd tried to explain that he was Diamond's Pappy Vic, and just Uncle Vic to the rest, but they refused to make the distinction. Pappy to one Fuzzy, pappy to all.

"Pappy Vic give *esteefee*," he told them. "New *estefee*, very good." He set the box down and got out one of the slabs, breaking and distributing it. The Fuzzies had nice manners; the two most recent guests, Pierrot and Columbine, served first, held theirs till the others were served. Then they all nibbled together.

They each took one nibble and stopped.

"Not good," Diamond declared. "Not *esteefee*. Want *esteefee*."

"Bad," Flora pronounced it, spitting out what she had in her mouth and carrying the rest to the trash-bin. "*Esteefee* good; this not."

"*Esteefee* for look; not *esteefee* in mouth," Pierrot said.

"What are they saying?" Dunbar wanted to know.

"They say it isn't Extee Three at all, and they want to know how dumb I am to think it is."

"But look, Mr. Grego; this *is* Extee Three. It is chemically identical with the stuff they've been eating all along."

"The Fuzzies aren't chemists. They only know what it tastes like, and it doesn't taste like Extee Three to them."

"It tastes like Extee Three to me . . ."

"You," Sandra told him, "are not a Fuzzy." She switched languages and explained that Pappy Vic and the other Big One really thought it was *esteefee*.

"Pappy Vic feel bad," he told them. "Pappy Vic want to give real esteefee."

He gathered up the offending carton and carried it into the kitchenette, going to one of the cupboards and getting out a tin of the genuine article. Only a dozen left; he'd have to start rationing it himself. He cut it into six pieces, put by a piece for Diamond after the company was gone, and distributed the rest.

Dunbar was still arguing with Sandra that the stuff he'd brought was chemically Extee Three.

"All right, Malcolm, I believe you. The point is, these Fuzzies don't give a hoot on Nifflheim what the chemical composition is." He looked at the label on the tin. "The man you have at the plant worked for Odin Dietetics, didn't he? Well, this stuff was made on Terra by Argentine Syntho-Foods. What do they use for cereal bulk-matter at Odin Dietetics, some native grain?"

"No, introduced Terran wheat, and Argentine uses wheat from the pampas and from the Mississippi Valley in North America."

"Different soil-chemicals, different bacteria; hell, man, look at tobacco. We've introduced it on every planet we've ever colonized, and no tobacco tastes just like the tobacco from anywhere else."

"Do we have any Odin Extee Three?" Sandra asked.

"Smart girl; a triple A for good thinking. Do we?"

"Yes. The stuff we import's Argentine, and the stuff the Navy has on Xerxes is Odin."

"And the Fuzzies can't tell the difference? No, of course they can't. Jack Holloway bought his Extee Three from us and gave it to his Fuzzies, and when they got on Xerxes, the Navy fed them theirs. What did you use in this stuff, local wheat?"

"Introduced wheat; seed came from South America. Grown on Gammz Continent."

"Well, Mal, we're going to find out what's the matter with this stuff. Real all-out study, tear it apart molecule by molecule. Who's our best biochemist?"

"Hoenveld."

"Well, put him to work on it. There's some difference, and the Fuzzies know it. You say this stuff's Government specification standard?"

"It meets the Government tests."

"Well; Napier has a lot of Extee Three on Xerxes he won't release because it's regulation-required emergency stores. We'll see if we can trade this for it . . ."

"Well, you goofed on it somehow!" the superintendent of the synthetics plant was insisting. "The Fuzzies eat regular Extee Three; they're crazy about it. If they won't eat your stuff, it isn't Extee Three."

"Listen, Abe, goddamit, I know it *is* Extee Three! We followed the formula exactly. Ask Joe Vespi, here; he used to work at Odin Dietetics . . ."

"That's correct, Mr. Fitch; every step of the process is exactly as I remember it from Odin—"

"*As you remembered it!*" Fitch pounced triumphantly. "What did you remember wrong?"

"Why, nothing, Mr. Fitch. Look, here's the schematic. The farina, that's the bulk-matter, comes in here, to these pressure-cookers . . ."

Dr. Jan Christiaan Hoenveld was annoyed, and because he was an emminent scientist and Victor Grego was only a businessman, he was at no pains to hide it.

"Mr. Grego, do you realize how much work is piled up on me now. Dr. Andrews and Dr. Reynier and Dr. Dosihara are at me to find out whether there is any biochemical cause of premature and defective births among Fuzzies. And now you want me to drop that and find out why one batch of Extee Three tastes differently to a Fuzzy from another. There is a gunsmith here in town who has a sign in his shop, *There are only*

twenty-four hours in a day and there is only one of me.
I have often considered copying that sign in my laboratory." He sat frowning into his screen from Science
Center, across the city, for a moment. "Mr. Grego, has
it occurred to you or any of your master-minds at
Synthetics that difference may be in the Fuzzies'
taste-perception?"

"It has occurred to me that Fuzzies must have a sense
of taste that would shame the most famous wine-taster
in the Galaxy. But I question if it is more accurate
than your chemical analysis. If those Fuzzies tasted a
difference between our Extee Three and Argentine Syn-
tho-Food's, the difference must be detectable. I don't
know anybody better able to detect it than you, Doctor; that's why I'm asking you to find out what it is."

Dr. Jan Christiaan Hoenveld said, "Hunnh!" ungra-
ciously. Flattered, and didn't want to show it.

"Well, I'll do what I can, Mr. Grego . . ."

XV

I must be very nice to Dr. Ernst Mallin. I must be very nice to Dr. Ernst Mallin. I must be . . . Ruth van Riebeek repeated it silently, as though writing it a hundred times on a mental blackboard, as the airboat lost altitude and came slanting down across the city, past the high crag of Company House, with the lower, broader, butte of Central Courts Building in the distance to the left. Ahead, the sanatorium area drew closer, wide parklands scattered with low white buildings. She hadn't seen Mallin since the trial, and even then she had avoided speaking to him as much as possible. Part of it was because of the things he had done with the four Fuzzies; Pancho Ybarra said she also had a guilt-complex because of the way she'd fifth-columned the company. Rubbish! That had been intelligence-work; that had been why she'd taken a job with the CZC in the first place. She had nothing at all to feel guilty about . . .

"I must be very nice to Dr. Ernst Mallin," she said, aloud. "And I'm going to have one Nifflheim of a time doing it."

"So am I," her husband, standing beside her, said.

"He'll have to make an effort to be nice to us, too. He'll still remember my pistol shoved into his back out at Holloway's the day Goldilocks was killed. I wonder if he knows how little it would have taken to make me squeeze the trigger."

"Pancho says he is a reformed character."

"Pancho's seen him since we have. He could be right. Anyhow, he's helping us, and we need all the help we can get. And he won't hurt the Fuzzies, not with Ahmed Khadra and Mrs. Pendarvis keeping an eye on him."

The Fuzzies, crowded on the cargo-deck below, were becoming excited. There was a forward-view screen rigged where they could see it, and they could probably sense as well as see that the boat was descending. And this place ahead must be the place Pappy Jack and Pappy Gerd and Unka Panko and Little Fuzzy had been telling them about, where the Big Ones would come and take them away to nice places of their own.

She hoped too many of them wouldn't be too badly disappointed. She hoped this adoption deal wouldn't be too much of a failure.

The airboat grounded on the vitrified stone apron beside the building. It looked like a good place; Jack said it had been intended for but never used as a mental ward-unit; four stories high, each with its own terrace, and a flat garden-planted roof. High mesh fences around each level; the Fuzzies wouldn't fall off. Plenty of trees and bushes; the Fuzzies would like that.

They got the Fuzzies off and into the building, helped by the small crowd who were waiting for them. Mrs. Pendarvis; she and the Chief Justice's wife were old friends. And a tall, red-haired girl, Grego's Fuzzy-sitter, Sandra Glenn. And Ahmed Khadra, in a new suit of civvies but bulging slightly under the left arm. And half a dozen other people whom she had met now and then —school department and company public health section. And Ernst Mallin, pompous and black-suited and pedantic-looking. *I must be very nice . . .* She extended a hand to him.

"Good afternoon, Dr. Mallin."

Maybe Gerd was right; maybe she did feel guilty about the way she'd tricked him. She was, she found, being counter-offensively defensive.

"Good afternoon, Ruth. Dr. van Riebeek," he corrected himself. "Can you bring your people down this way?" he asked, nodding to the hundred and fifty Fuzzies milling about in the hall, yeeking exictedly. People, he called them. He must be making an effort, too. "We have refreshments for them. Extee Three. And things for them to play with."

"Where do you get the Extee Three?" she asked. "We haven't been able to get any for almost a week, now."

Mallin gave one of his little secretive smiles, the sort he gave when he was one up on somebody.

"We got it from Xerxes. The company's started producing it, but unfortunately, the Fuzzies don't like it. We still can't find out why; it's made on exactly the same formula. And as it's entirely up to Government specifications, Mr. Grego was able to talk Commodore Napier into accepting it in exchange for what he has on hand. We have about five tons of it. How much do you need at Holloway's Camp? Will a couple of tons help you any?"

Would a couple of tons help them any? "Why, I don't know how to thank you, Dr. Mallin! Of course it will; we've been giving it to our Fuzzies, a quarter-cake apiece on alternate days." *I must be very,* VERY, *nice to Dr. Mallin!* "Why don't they like the stuff you people have been making? What's wrong with it?"

"We don't know. Mr. Grego has been raging at everybody to find out; it's made in exactly the same way . . ."

When Malcolm Dunbar lighted his screen, Dr. Jan Christiaan Hoenveld appeared in it. He didn't waste time on greetings or other superfluities.

"I think we have something, Mr. Dunbar. There is a component in both the Odin Dietetics and the Argentine Syntho-Foods products that is absent from our own product. It is not one of the synthetic nutrient or vitamin or hormone compounds which are part of the field-ration formula, it is not a compound regularly synthesized, either commercially or experimentally in any laboratory I know of. It's a rather complicated long-chain organic molecule; most of it seems to be oxygen-hydrogen-carbon, but there are a few atoms of titanium in it. If that's what the Fuzzies find lacking in our products, all I can say is that they have the keenest taste perception of any creature, sapient or non-sapient, that I have ever heard of."

"All right, then; they have. I saw them reject our Extee Three in disgust, and then Mr. Grego gave them a little of the Argentine stuff, and they ate it with the greatest pleasure. How much of this unknown compound is there in Extee Three?"

"About one part in ten thousand," Hoenveld said.

"And the titanium?"

"Five atoms out of sixty-four in the molecule."

"That's pretty keen tasting." He thought for a moment. "I suppose it's in the wheat; the rest of that stuff is synthesized."

"Well, naturally, Mr. Dunbar. That would seem

to be the inescapable conclusion," Hoenveld said, patronizingly.

"We have quite a bit of metallic titanium, imported in fabricated form before we got our own steel-mills working. Do you think you could synthesize that molecule, Dr. Hoenveld?"

Hoenveld gave him a look of undisguised contempt. "Certainly, Mr. Dunbar. In about a year and a half to two years. As I understand, the object of manufacturing the stuff here is to supply a temporary shortage which will be relieved in about six months, when imported Extee Three begins coming in from Marduk. Unless I am directly and specifically ordered to do so by Mr. Grego, I will not waste my time on trying."

Of course, it was ending in a cocktail party. Wherever Terran humans went, they planted tobacco and coffee, to have coffee and cigarettes for breakfast, and wherever they went they found or introduced something that would ferment to produce C_2H_5OH, and around 1730-ish each day, they had Cocktail Hour. The natives on planets like Loki and Gimli and Thor and even Shesha and Uller thought it was a religious observance.

Maybe it was, at that.

Sipping his own cocktail, Gerd van Riebeek ignored, for a moment, the conversation in which he had become involved and eavesdropped on his wife and Claudette Pendarvis and Ernst Mallin and Ahmed Khadra and Sandra Glenn.

"Well, we want to keep them here for at least a week before we let people take them away," the Chief Justice's wife was saying. "You'll have to stay with us for a day or so, Ruth, and help us teach them what to expect in their new homes."

"You're going to have to educate the people who adopt them," Sandra Glenn said. "What to expect and what not to expect from Fuzzies. I think, evening classes. Language, for one thing."

"You know," Mallin said, "I'd like to take a few Fuzzies around through the other units of the sanatorium, to visit the patients. The patients here would like it. They don't have an awful lot of fun, you know."

That was new for Ernst Mallin. He never seemed to recall that Mallin had thought having fun was important, before. Maybe the Fuzzies had taught him that it was.

The group he was drinking with were Science Center and Public Health people. One of them, a woman gynecologist, was wondering what Chris Hoenveld had found out, so far.

"What can he find out?" Raynier, the pathologist asked. "He only has the one specimen, and it probably isn't there at all, it's probably something in the mother's metabolism. It might be radioactivity, but that would only produce an occasional isolated case, and from what you've seen, it seems to be a racial characteristic. I think you'll find it in the racial dietary habits."

"Land-prawns," somebody suggested. "As far as I know, nothing else eats them but Fuzzies; that right, Gerd?"

"Yes. We always thought they had no natural enemies at all, till we found out about the Fuzzies. But it's been our observation that Fuzzies won't take anything that'll hurt them."

"They won't take anything that gives them a bellyache or a hangover, no. They can establish a direct relationship there. But whatever caused this defective birth we were investigating, and I agree that that's probably a common thing with Fuzzies, was something that acted on a level the Fuzzies couldn't be aware of. I think there's a good chance that eating land-prawns may be responsible."

"Well, let's find out. Put Chris Hoenveld to work on that."

"You put him to work on it. Or get Victor Grego to; he won't throw Grego out of his lab. Chris is sore enough about this Fuzzy business as it is."

"Well, we'll have to study more than one fetus. We have a hundred and fifty Fuzzies here, we ought to find something out . . .

"Isolate all the pregnant females; get Mrs. Pendarvis to withhold them from adoption. . . ."

". . . may have to perform a few abortions . . ."

". . . microsurgery; fertilized ova . . ."

That wasn't what he and Ruth and Jack Holloway had had in mind, when they'd brought this lot to Mallorysport. But they had to find out; if they didn't, in a few more generations there might be no more Fuzzies at all. If a few of them suffered, now . . .

Well, hadn't poor Goldilocks had to be killed before the Fuzzies were recognized for the people they were?

"Titanium," Victor Grego said. "Now that's interesting."

"Is that all you can call it, Mr. Grego?" Dunbar, in the screen, demanded. "I call it impossible. I was checking up. Titanium, on this planet, is damn near as rare as calcium on Uller. It's present, and that's all; I'll bet most of the titanium on Zarathustra was brought here in fabricated form between the time the planet was discovered and seven years ago when we got our steel-mill going."

That was a big exaggeration, of course. It existed, but it was a fact that they'd never been able to extract it by any commercially profitable process, and on Zarathustra they used light-alloy steel for everything for which titanium was used elsewhere. So a little of it got picked up, as a trace-element, in wheat grown on Terra or on Odin, but it was useless to hope for it in Zarathustran wheat.

"It looks," he said, "as though we're stuck, Mal. Do you think Chris Hoenveld could synthesize that molecule? We could add it to the other ingredients..."

"He says he could—in six months to a year. He refuses to try unless you order him categorically to."

"And by that time, we'll have all the Extee Three we want. Well, a lot of Fuzzies, including mine, are going to have to do without, then."

He blanked the screen and lit a cigarette and looked at the globe of Zarathustra, which Henry Stenson had running on time again and which he could interpret like a clock. Be another hour till Sandra got back from the new Adoption Center; she'd have to pick up Diamond at Government House. And Leslie wouldn't be in for cocktails this evening; he was over on Epsilon Continent, talking to people about things he didn't want to discuss by screen. Ben Rainsford had finally gotten around to calling for an election for delegates to a constitutional convention, and they wanted to line up candidates of their own. It looked as though Mr. Victor Grego would have cocktails with the manager-in-chief of the Charterless Zarathustra Company, this evening. Might as well have them here.

Titanium, he thought disgustedly. It would be something like that. What was it they called the stuff? Oh, yes; the nymphomaniac metal; when it gets hot it com-

bines with anything. An idea suddenly danced just out
of reach. He stopped, half way from the desk to the
cabinet, his eyes closed. Then he caught it, and dashed
for the communication screen, punching Malcolm Dunbar's call-combination.

It was a few minutes before Dunbar answered; he
had his hat and coat on.

"I was just going out, Mr. Grego."

"So I see. That man Vespi, the one who worked for
Odin Dietetics; is he still around?"

"Why, no. He left twenty minutes ago, and I don't
know how to reach him, right away."

"No matter; get him in the morning. Listen, the pressure cookers, the ones you use to cook the farina for
bulk-matter. What are they made of?"

"Why, light nonox-steel; our manufacture. Why?"

"Ask Vespi what they used for that purpose on Odin.
Don't suggest the answer, but see if it wasn't titanium."

Dunbar's eyes widened. He'd heard about the chemical nymphomania of titanium, too.

"Sure; that's what they'd use, there. And at Argentine
Syntho-Foods, too. Listen, suppose I give the police an
emergency-call request; they could find Joe in half an
hour."

"Don't bother; tomorrow morning's good enough. I
want to try something first."

He blanked the screen, and called Myra Fallada. She
never left the office before he did.

"Myra; call out and get me five pounds of pure wheat
farina, and be sure it's made from Zarathustran wheat.
Have it sent up to my apartment, fifteen minutes ago."

"Fifteen minutes from now do?" she asked. "What's
it for; the Little Monster? All right, Mr. Grego."

He forgot about the drink he was going to have with

Mr. Victor Grego. You had a drink when the work was done, and there was still work to do.

There was clattering in the kitchenette when Sandra Glenn brought Diamond into the Fuzzy-room. She opened the door between and looked through, and Diamond crowded past her knees for a look, too. Mr. Grego was cooking something, in a battered old stewpan she had never seen around the place before. He looked over his shoulder and said, "Hi, Sandra. *Heyo,* Diamond; use Fuzzyphone, Pappy Vic no got ear-thing."

"What make do, Pappy Vic?" Diamond asked.

"That's what I want to know, too?"

"Sandra, keep your fingers crossed; when this stuff's done and has cooled off, we're going to see how Diamond likes it. I think we have found out what's the matter with that Extee Three."

"*Esteefee?* You make *esteefee?* Real? Not like other?" Diamond wanted to know.

"You eat," Pappy Vic said. "Tell if good. Pappy Vic not know."

"Well, what is it?" she asked.

"Hoenveld found what was different about it." The explanation was rather complicated; she had been exposed to, rather than studied, chemistry. She got the general idea; the Extee Three the Fuzzies liked had been cooked in titanium.

"That's what this stewpan is; part of a camp cooking kit I brought here from Terra." He gave the white mess in the pan a final stir and lifted it from the stove, burning his finger and swearing; just like a man in a kitchen. "Now, as soon as this slop's cool . . ."

Diamond smelled it, and wanted to try it right away. He had to wait, though, until it was cool. Then they carried the pan, it had a treacherous-looking folding handle, out to the Fuzzy-room, and Mr. Grego spooned some onto Diamond's plate, and Diamond took his little spoon and tasted, cautiously. Then he began shoveling it into his mouth ravenously.

"The Master Mind crashes through again," she said. "He really likes it." Diamond had finished what was on his plate. "You like?" she asked, in Fuzzy. "Want more?"

"Give him the rest of it, Sandra. I'm going to call Dr. Jan Christiaan Hoenveld, and suggest an experiment for him to try. And after that, Miss Glenn, will you honor me by having a cocktail with me?"

Jack Holloway laughed. "So that's it. When did you find out?"

"Mallin just screened me; he just got it from Grego," Gerd van Riebeek, in the screen, said. "They're going to start tearing out all the stainless-steel cookers right away, and replace them with titanium. Jack, have you any titanium cooking utensils?"

"No. Everything we have here is steel. We have sheet titanium; the house and the sheds and the old hangar are all sheet-titanium. We might be able to make something . . ." He stopped short. "Gerd, we don't have to cook the food in titanium. We can cook titanium in the food. Cut up some chunks and put them in the kettles. It would work the same way."

"Well, I'll be damned," Gerd said. "I never thought of that. I'll bet nobody else did, either."

Dr. Jan Christiaan Hoenveld was disgusted and chagrined and embarrassed, and mostly disgusted.

It had been gratifying to discover a hitherto unknown biochemical, especially one existing unsuspected in a well known, long manufactured, and widely distributed commercial product. He could understand how it had happened; a by-effect in one of the manufacturing processes, and since the stuff had been proven safe and nutritious for humans and other life-forms having similar biochemistry and metabolism, nobody had bothered until some little animals—no, people, that had been scientifically established—had detected its absence by taste. Things like that happened all the time. He had been proud of the accomplishment; he'd been going to call the newly discovered substance hoenveldine. He could have worked out a way of synthesizing it, too, but by proper scientific methods it would have taken over a year, and he knew it, and he'd said so to everybody.

And now, within a day, it had been synthesized, if that were the word for it, by a rank amateur, a layman, a complete non-scientist. And not in a laboratory in a kitchen, with no equipment but a battered old stewpan!

And the worst of it was that this layman, this empiric, was his employer. The claims of the manager-in-chief of the Zarathustra Company simply couldn't be brushed off. Not by a company scientist.

Well, Grego had found out what he wanted; he could stop worrying about that. He had important work to do; an orderly, long-term study of the differences between Zarathustran and Terran biochemistry. The differences were minute, but they existed, and they had to be understood, and they had to be investigated in an orderly, scientific manner.

And now, they wanted him to go haring off, hit-or-miss, after this problem about Fuzzy infant mortality and defective births, and they didn't even know any

such problem existed. They had one, just one, case—
that six-month fetus the Andrews girl had brought in—
and they had a lot of unsubstantiated theorizing by
Gerd van Riebeek, pure conclusion-jumping. And now
they wanted him to find out if eating land-prawns
caused these defective births which they believed, on the
basis of one case and a lot of supposition, to exist.
Maybe after years of observation of hundreds of cases
they might have some justification, but . . .

He rose from the chair at the desk in the corner of
the laboratory and walked slowly among the work-
benches. Ten men and women, eight of them working
on new projects that had been started since young van
Riebeek had started after this mare's-nest of his, all of
them diverted from serious planned research. He stopped
at one bench, where a woman was working.

"Miss Tresca, can't you keep your bench in better
order than this?" he scolded. "Keep things in their
places. What are you working on?"

"Oh, a hunch I had, about this hokfusine."

Hunch! That was the trouble, all through Science
Center; too many hunches and not enough sound theory.

"Oh, the titanium thing. It's a name Mr. Grego suggested, from a couple of Fuzzy words, *hoku fusso,* wonderful food. It's what the Fuzzies call Extee Three."

Hokfusine, indeed. Now they were getting the Fuzzy
language into scientific nomenclature.

"Well, just forget about your hunch," he told her.
"There are a lot of samples of organic matter, blood,
body-secretions, hormones, tissue, from pregnant female
Fuzzies that they want analyzed. I don't suppose it
makes any more sense than your hunch, but they want
analyses immediately. They want everything immediately, it seems. And straighten up that clutter on your

bench. How often do I have to tell you that order is the first virtue in scientific work?"

XVI

THEY were in Jack's living room, and it looked almost exactly as it had the first night Gerd van Riebeek had seen it, when he and Ruth and Juan Jimenez had come out to see the Fuzzies, without the least idea that the validity of the company's charter would be involved. All the new office equipment that had cluttered it had gone, in the two weeks he and Ruth had been in Mallorysport, and there was just the sturdy, comfortable furniture Jack had made himself, and the damnthing and the bush-goblin and veldbeest skins on the floor, and the gunrack with the tangle of bedding under it.

There were just five of them, as there had been that other evening, three months, or was it three ages, ago. Juan Jimenez and Ben Rainsford were absent, in Mallorysport, but they had been replaced by Pancho Ybarra, lounging in one of the deep chairs, and Lynne Andrews, on the couch beside Ruth. Jack sat in the armchair at his table-desk, trying to keep Baby Fuzzy, on his lap, from climbing up to sit on his head. On the floor, the adult Fuzzies—just Jack's own family; this was their place, and the others didn't intrude here —were in the middle of the room, playing with the things that had been brought back from Mallorysport. The kind of playthings Fuzzies liked; ingenuity-challenging toys for putting together shapes and colors.

He was glad they weren't playing with their molecule-model kit. He'd seen enough molecule models in the last two weeks to last him a lifetime.

"And there isn't anything we can do about it, at all?" Lynne was asking.

"No. There isn't anything anybody can do. The people in Mallorysport have given up trying. They're still investigating, but that's only to be able to write a scientifically accurate epitaph for the Fuzzy race."

"Can't they do something to reverse it?"

"It's irreversible," Ruth told her. "It isn't a matter of diet or environment or anything external. It's this hormone, NFMp, that they produce in their own bodies, that inhibits normal development of the embryo. And we can't even correct it in individual cases by surgery; excising the glands that secrete it would result in sterility."

"Well, it doesn't always work," Jack said, lifting Baby Fuzzy from his shoulder. "It didn't work in Baby's case."

"It works in about nine cases out of ten, apparently. We've had ten births so far; one normal and healthy, and the rest premature and defective, stillbirths, or live births that die within hours."

"But there are exceptions, Baby here, and the one over at the Fuzzy-shelter," Lynne said. "Can't we figure out how the exceptions can be encouraged?"

"They're working on that, in a half-hearted way," he told her. "Fuzzies have a menstrual cycle and fertility rhythm, the same as *Homo s. terra,* and apparently the NFMp output is also cyclic, and when the two are out of phase there is a normal viable birth, and not otherwise. And this doesn't happen often enough, and any correction of it would have to be done individually in the case of each female Fuzzy, and nobody even knows how to find out how it could be done."

"But, Gerd, the whole thing doesn't make sense to me," Pancho objected. "I know, 'sense' is nothing but ignorance rationalized, and this isn't my subject, but if this NFMp thing is a racial characteristic, it must be hereditary, and a hereditary tendency to miscarriages premature and defective births, and infant mortality, now; what kind of sense does that make?"

"Well, on the face of it, not much. But we know nothing at all about the racial history of the Fuzzies, and very little about the history of this planet. Say that fifty thousand years ago there were millions of Fuzzies, and say that fifty thousand years ago environmental conditions were radically different. This NMFp hormone was evolved to meet some environmental survival demand, and something in the environment, some article of diet that has now vanished, kept it from injuriously affecting the unborn Fuzzies. Then the environment changed—glaciation, glacial recession, sea-level fluctuation, I can think of dozens of reasons—and after having adapted to original conditions, they couldn't re-adapt to the change. We've seen it on every planet we've ever studied; hundreds of cases on Terra alone. The Fuzzies are just caught in a genetic trap they can't get out of, and we can't get them out of it."

He looked at them; six happy little people, busily fitting many-colored jointed blocks together to make a useless and delightful pretty-thing. Happy in ignorance of their racial doom.

"If we knew how many children the average female

has in her lifetime, and how many child-bearers there are, we could figure it out mathematically, I suppose. Ten little Fuzzies, nine little Fuzzies, eight little Fuzzies, and finally no little Fuzzies."

Little Fuzzy thought he was being talked about; he looked up inquiringly.

"Well, they won't all just vanish in the next minute," Jack said. "I expect this gang'll attend my funeral, and there'll be Fuzzies as long as any of you live, and longer. In a couple of million years, there won't be any more humans, I suppose. Let's just be as good to the Fuzzies we have as we can, and make them as happy as possible . . . Yes, Baby; you can sit on Pappy's head if you want to."

XVII

THE best time for telecast political speeches was between 2000 and 2100, when people were relaxing after dinner and before they started going out or before guests began to arrive. That was a little late for Beta Continent and impossibly so for Gamma, but Delta and Epsilon, to the west, could be reached with late night repeats and about eighty percent of the planetary population was concentrated here on Alpha Continent. Of late, Hugo Ingermann had been having trouble getting on the air at that time. The 2000-2100 spot, he was always told, was already booked, and it would usually turn out to be by the Citizen's Government League which everybody knew but nobody could prove was masterminded by Leslie Coombes and Victor Grego, or it would be Ben Rainsford trying to alibi his Government, or by a lecture on the care and feeding of Fuzzies. But this time, somebody had goofed. This time, he'd been able to get the 2000-2100 spot himself. The voice of the announcer at the telecast station came out of the sound-outlet:

". . . an important message, to all the citizens of the Colony, now, by virtue of the Pendarvis Decisions, enjoying, for the first time, the right of democratic self-government. The next voice you will hear will be that of the Honorable Hugo Ingermann, organizer and leader of the Planetary Prosperity Party. Mr. Ingermann."

The green light came on, and the showback lightened; he lifted his hand in greeting.

"My ... *friends!*" he began.

Frederic Pendarvis was growing coldly angry. It wasn't an organizational abstraction, the Native Adoption Bureau, that was being attacked; it was his wife, Claudette, and he was taking it personally, and a judge should never take anything personally. Why, he had actually been looking at the plump, bland-faced man in the screen, his blue eyes wide with counterfeit sincerity, and wondering whom to send to him with a challenge. Dueling wasn't illegal on Zarathustra, it wasn't on most of the newer planets, but judges did not duel.

And the worst of it, he thought, was that the next time he had to rule against Ingermann in court, Ingermann would be sure, by some innuendo which couldn't be established as overt contempt, to create an impression that it was due to personal vindicativeness.

"It is a disgraceful record," Ingermann was declaring. "A record reeking with favoritism, inequity, class prejudice. In all, twelve hundred applications have been received. Over two hundred have been rejected outright, often on the most frivolous and insulting grounds ..."

"Mental or emotional instability, inability to support or care for a Fuzzy, irresponsibility, bad character, undesirable home conditions," Claudette, who was beginning to become angry herself, mentioned.

Pierrot and Columbine, on the floor, with a big Mobius strip somebody had made from a length of tape, looked up quickly and then, deciding that it was the man in the wall Mummy was mad at, went back to trying to figure out where the other side always went.

"And of the thousand applications, only three hundred and forty-five have been filled, although five hundred and sixty-six Fuzzies have been brought to this city since the Adoption Bureau was opened. One hundred and seventy-two of these applicants have received a Fuzzy each. One hundred and fifty-five have received two Fuzzies each. And eighteen especially favored ones have received a total of eighty-four Fuzzies.

"And almost without exception, all these Fuzzies have gone to socially or politically prominent persons, persons of wealth. You might as well make up your mind to it, a poor man has no chance whatever. Look who all have gotten Fuzzies under the Fuzzy laws, if one may so term the edicts of a bayonet-imposed Governor. The first papers of adoption were issued to—guess who now?—Victor Grego, the manager-in-chief of the now Charterless Zarathustra Company. And the next pair went to Mrs. Frederic Pendarvis, and beside being the Chief Justice's wife, who is she? Why, the head of the Adoption Bureau, of course. And look at the rest of these names! Nine tenths of them are Zarathustra Company executives." He held up his hands, as though to hush an outburst of righteous indignation. "Now I won't claim, I won't even suppose, that there is any actual corruption or any bribery about this . . ."

"You damned well better hadn't! If you do, I won't sue you, I'll shoot you," Pendarvis barked.

"I won't do either," his wife told him calmly. "But I will answer him. Under veridication, and that's something Hugo Ingermann would never dare do."

"Claudette!" He was shocked. "You wouldn't do that? Not on telecast?"

"On telecast. You can't ignore this sort of thing. If you do, you just admit it by default. There's only one answer to slander, and that's to prove the truth."

"And who's paying for all this?" Ingermann demanded out of the screen. "The Government? When Space Commodore Napier presented us with this Government, and this Governor, at pistol point, there was exactly half a million sols to the account of the Colony in the Bank of Mallorysport. Since then, Governor Rainsford has borrowed approximately half a *billion* sols from the Banking Cartel. And how is Ben Rainsford going to repay them? By taking it out of you and me and all of us, as soon as he can get a Colonial Legislature to rubber-stamp his demands for him. And now, do you know what he is spending millions of your money on? On a project to increase the Fuzzy birthrate, so that you'll have more and more Fuzzies for his friends to make pets of and for you to pay the bills for . . ."

"He is a God damned unmitigated liar!" Victor Grego said. "Except for a little work Ruth Ortheris and her husband and Pancho Ybarra and Lynne Andrews are doing out at Holloway's, the company's paying for all that infant mortality research, and I'll have to justify it to the stockholders."

"How about some publicity on that?" Coombes asked. "You're the political expert; what do you think?"

"I think it would help. I think it would help us, and I think it would help Rainsford. Let's not do it ourselves, though. Suppose I talk to Gus Brannhard, and have him advise Jack Holloway to leak it to the press?"

"Press is going to be after Mrs. Pendarvis for a statement. She knows what the facts are. Let her tell it."

"He make talk about Fuzzies?" Diamond, who had been watching Hugo Ingermann fascinatedly, inquired.

"Yes. Not like Fuzzies. Bad Big One; *tosh-ki Hagga.* Pappy Vic not like him."

"Neither," Coombes said, "does Unka Leslie."

Ahmed Khadra blew cigarette smoke insultingly at the face in the screen. Hugo Ingermann was saying:

"Well, if few politicians and company executives are getting all the Fuzzies, why not make them pay for it, instead of the common people of the planet? Why not charge a fee for adoption papers, say five hundred to a thousand sols? Everybody who's gotten Fuzzies so far could easily pay that. It wouldn't begin to meet the cost of maintaining the Native Affairs Commission, but it would be something..."

So that was what the whole thing had been pointed toward. Make it expensive to adopt Fuzzies legally. A black market couldn't compete with free Fuzzies, but let the Adoption Bureau charge five hundred sols apiece for them...

"So that's what you're after, you son of a Khooghra? A competitive market."

XVIII

"You got this from one of my laboratory workers," Jan Christiaan Hoenveld accused. "Charlotte Tresca, wasn't it?"

He was calling from his private cubical in the corner of the biochemistry lab; through the glass partition behind him Juan Jimenez could see people working at benches, including, he thought, his informant. For the moment, he disregarded the older man's tone and manner.

"That's correct, Dr. Hoenveld. I met Miss Tresca at a cocktail party last evening. She and some other Science Center people were discussing the different phases of the Fuzzy research, and she mentioned having found hokfusine, or something very similar to it, in the digestive tracts of land-prawns. That had been a week ago; she had reported her findings to you immediately, and assumed that you had reported them to me. Now, I want to know why you didn't."

"Because it wasn't worth reporting," Hoenveld snapped. "In the first place, she wasn't supposed to be working on land-prawns, or hokfusine,"—he almost spat the word in contempt — "at all. She was supposed to be looking for NFMp in this mess of guts and tripes you've been dumping into my laboratory from all over the planet. And in the second place, it was merely a trace-presence of titanium, with which she had probably contaminated the test herself. The girl is an incurably careless and untidy worker. And finally," Hoenveld raged, "I want to know by what right you question my laboratory workers behind my back..."

"Oh, you do? Well, they are not *your* laboratory workers, Dr. Hoenveld; they are employees of the Zarathustra Company, the same as you. Or I. And the biochemistry laboratory is not your private empire. It is a part of Science Center, of which I am division chief, and from where I sit the difference between you and Charlotte Tresca is barely perceptible to the naked eye. Is that clear, Dr. Hoenveld?"

Hoenveld was looking at him as though a pistol had blown up in his hand. He was, in fact, mildly surprised at himself. A month ago, he wouldn't have dreamed of talking so to anybody, least of all a man as much older than himself as Hoenveld, and one with Hoenveld's imposing reputation.

But as division chief, he had to get things done, and there could be only one chief in the division.

"I am quite well aware of your recent and sudden promotion, Dr. Jimenez," Hoenveld retorted acidly. "Over the heads of a dozen of your seniors."

"Including yourself; well, you've just demonstrated the reason why you were passed over. Now, I want some work done, and if you can't or won't do it, I can promote somebody to replace you very easily."

"What do you think we've been doing? Every ranger and hunter on the company payroll has been shooting everything from damnthings and wild veldbeest to ground-mice and dumping the digestive and reproductive tracts in my — I beg your pardon, I mean the Charterless Zarathustra Company's — laboratory."

"Have you found any trace of NFMp in any of them?"

"Negative. They don't have the glands to secrete it; I have that on the authority of the comparative mammalian anatomists."

"Then stop looking for it; I'll order the specimen collecting stopped at once. Now, I want analyses of land-prawns made, and I want to know just what Miss Tresca found in them; whether it was really hokfusine, or anything similar to it, or just trace-presences of titanium, and I want to know how it gets into the land-prawns' systems and where it concentrates there. I would suggest — correction, I direct — that Miss Tresca be put to work on that herself, and that she report directly to me."

"What's your opinion of Chris Hoenveld, Ernst?" Victor Grego asked.

Mallin frowned — his standard think-seriously-and-weigh-every-word frown.

"Dr. Hoenveld is a most distinguished scientist. He has an encyclopediac grasp on his subject, an infallible memory, and an infinite capacity for taking pains."

"Is that all?"

"Isn't that enough?"

"No. A computer has all that, to a much higher degree, and a computer couldn't make an original scientific discovery in a hundred million years. A computer has no imagination, and neither has Hoenveld."

"Well, he has very little, I'll admit. Why do you ask about him?"

"Juan Jimenez is having trouble with him."

"I can believe it," Mallin said. "Hoenveld has one

characteristic a computer lacks. Egotism. Has Jimenez complained to you?"

"Nifflheim, no; he's running Science Center without yelling to Big Brother for help. I got this off the powder-room and coffee-stand telegraph, to which I have excellent taps. Juan cut him down to size; he's doing all right."

"Well, how about the NFMp problem?"

"Nowhere, on hyperdrive. The Fuzzies just manufacture it inside themselves, and nobody knows why. It seems mainly to be associated with the digestive system, and gets from there into the blood-stream, and into the gonads, in both sexes, from there. Thirty-six births, so far; three viable."

From the terrace outside came the happy babble of Fuzzy voices. They were using their Fuzzyphones to talk to one another; wanted to talk like the Hagga. Poor little tail-enders of a doomed race.

The whole damned thing was getting too big for comfort, Jack Holloway thought. A month ago, there'd only been Gerd and Ruth and Lynne Andrews and Pancho Ybarra, and George Lunt, and the men George had brought when he'd transferred from the Constabulary. They all had cocktails together before dinner, and ate at one table, and had bull-sessions in the evenings, and everybody had known what everybody else was doing. And there had only been forty or fifty Fuzzies, beside his and George's and Gerd's and Ruth's.

Now Gerd had three assistants, and Ruth had dropped work on Fuzzy psychology and was helping him with whatever he was doing, and what that was he wasn't quite sure. He wasn't quite sure what anybody was doing, any more. And Pancho was practically commuting to and from Mallorysport, and Ernst Mallin was out at least once a week. Funny, too; he used to think Mallin was a solid, three-dimensional bastard, and now he found he rather liked him. Even Victor Grego was out, one week-end, and everybody liked him.

Lynne had a couple of helpers, too, and a hospital and clinic, and there was a Fuzzy school, where they were taught Lingua Terra and how to use Fuzzyphones and about the strange customs of the Hagga. Some old hen Ruth had kidnapped from the Mallorysport schools was in charge of it, or thought she was; actually Little Fuzzy and Ko-Ko and Cinderella and Lizzie Borden and Dillinger were running it.

And he and George Lunt couldn't yell back and forth to each other any more, because their offices, at opposite ends of the long hut, were partitioned off and separated by a hundred and twenty feet of middle office, full of desks and business machines and roboclerks, and humans working with them. And he had a secretary, now, and she had a secretary, or at least a stenographer, of her own.

Gerd van Riebeek came in from the outside, tossing his hat on top of a microbook-case and unbuckling his pistol.

"Hi, Jack. Anything new?" he asked.

Gerd and Ruth had been away for a little over a week, in the country to the south. It must have been fun, just the two of them and Complex and Superego and Dr. Crippen and Calamity Jane, camping in Gerd's airboat and visiting the posts Lunt had strung out along the edge of the big woods.

"I was going to ask you that. Where's Ruth?"

"She's staying another week, at the Kirtland plantation, with Superego and Complex; there must be fifty to seventy-five Fuzzies there; she's helping the Kirtland people with them, teaching them not to destroy young sugarplant shoots. Kirtland's been taking a lot of damage to his shoots from zatku. What's the latest from Mallorysport?"

"Well, nowhere on the NFMp, but they seem to have found something interesting about the land-prawns."

"More on that?" Gerd had heard about the alleged hokfusine. "Have they found out what it is?"

"It isn't hokfusine, it's just a rather complicated titanium salt. The land-prawns eat titanium, mostly in moss and fungus and stuff like that. It probably grades about ten atoms to the ton on what they eat. But they fix it, apparently in that middle intestine that they have. I have a big long writeup on what it does there. The Fuzzies seem to convert it to something else in their own digestive system. Whatever it does, hokfusine seems to do it a lot better. They're still working on it."

"They ate land-prawns all along, but it was only since this new generation hatched, this Spring, that they really got all they wanted of them. I wonder what they ate before, up north."

"Well, we know what all they eat beside zatku and the stuff we give them. Animals small enough to kill with those little sticks, fruit, bird-eggs, those little yellow lizards, grubs."

"What are Paine's Marines doing up north now, beside looking for non-existent Fuzzy-catchers?"

"That's about all. Flying patrol, taking photos, mapping. They say there are lots of Fuzzies north of the Divide that haven't started south yet, probably haven't heard about the big zatku bonanza yet."

"I'm going up there, Jack. I want to look at them, see what they live on."

"Don't go right away; wait a week, and I'll go along with you. I still have a lot of this damn stuff to clear up, and I have to go in to Mallorysport tomorrow. Casagra's talking about recalling Paine and his men and vehicles. You know where that would put us."

Gerd nodded. "We'd have to double the ZNPF. It's all George can do to maintain those posts along the edge of the big woods and fly inspections in the farm country, without having to patrol in the north too."

"I don't know how we could pay or equip them, even if we could recruit them. We're operating on next year's budget now. That's another thing I'll have to talk to Ben about. He'll have to allocate us more money."

"God damn it, there's no money to give him!"

Ben Rainsford spoke aloud and bitterly, and then caught himself and puffed furiously on his pipe, the smoke reddening in the sunset afterglow. Have to watch that; people hear him talking to himself, it would be all over Government House, and all over Mallorysport in the next day, that Governor Rainsford was going crazy. Not that it would be any wonder if he were.

The three Fuzzies, Flora and Fauna and their friend Diamond, who had gotten hold of a lot of wooden strips of the sort the gardeners used for trelliswork and were building a little arbor of their own, looked up quickly and then realized that he wasn't speaking to them and went on with what they were doing. The sun had gone to bed already, and the sky-light was fading, and they wanted to get whatever it was they were making finished before it got dark. Fuzzies, like Colonial Governors, found time running out on them occasionally.

Time was running out fast for him. The ninety days the CZC had allowed him to take over all the public services they were no longer obliged to maintain were more than half gone now, and nothing had been done. The election for delegates to a constitutional convention was still a month in the future, and he had no idea how long it would take the elected delegates, whoever they'd be, to argue out a constitution, and how long thereafter it would take to get a Colonial Legislature set up, and how long after tax laws were enacted it would be before the Government would begin collecting money.

He wished he'd been able to borrow that half billion sols from the Banking Cartel that Hugo Ingermann had been yakking about. Ingermann had later been forced to back down to something closer the actual figure of fifty million, just as he had been forced to retreat from some of his exaggerated statements about the Adoption Bureau, but it seemed that the public still believed his original statements and were disregarding the hedging and weasel-worded retractions. Fifty million sounded like a lot of money, too — till you had to run a planetary government on it, and everything was going to cost so much more than he had expected.

The Native Affairs Commission, for instance. He and Jack had both believed that a hundred and fifty men would be ample for the Native Protection Force; now they were finding that three times that number wouldn't be enough. They had thought that Gerd and Ruth van Riebeek and Lynne Andrews, and Pancho Ybarra, on loan from the Navy, would be able to do all the study and research work; now that was spread out to Mallorysport Hospital and Science Center, for which the CZC was paying and would expect compensation. And the Adoption Bureau was costing as much, now, as the whole original Native Affairs Commission estimate.

At least, he'd been able to do one thing for Jack. Alex Napier had agreed that protection and/or policing of natives on Class-IV planets was a proper function of the Armed Forces, and instead of recalling his fifty men, Casagra had been ordered to reenforce them with twenty more.

The Fuzzies suddenly stopped what they were doing and turned. Diamond drew his Fuzzyphone. "Pappy Vic!" he called, in delighted surprise. "Come; look what we make!" Flora and Fauna were whooping greetings, too.

He rose, and saw behind him the short, compactly-built man, familiar from news-screen views, whom he had so far avoided meeting personally. Victor Grego greeted the Fuzzies, and then said, "Good evening, Governor. Sorry to intrude, but Miss Glenn has a dinner-and-dancing date, and I told her I'd get Diamond myself."

"Good evening, Mr. Grego." Somehow, he didn't feel the hostility to the man that he had expected. "Could you wait a little while? They have an important project, here, and they want to finish it while there's still daylight."

"Well, so I see." Grego spoke to the Fuzzies in their own language, and listened while they explained what they were doing. "Of course; we can't interfere with that."

The Fuzzies went back to their trellis-building. He and Grego sat down in lawn-chairs; Grego lit a cigarette. He watched the CZC manager-in-chief as the latter sat watching the Fuzzies. This couldn't be Victor Grego; "Victor Grego" was a label for a personification of black-hearted villainy and ruthless selfishness; this was a pleasant-spoken, courteous gentleman who loved Fuzzies, and was considerate of his employees.

"Miss Glenn's date was with Captain Ahmed Khadra," Grego was saying, to make conversation. "The fifth in the last two weeks. I'm afraid I'm just before losing a good Fuzzy-sitter by marriage."

"I'm afraid so; they seem quite serious about each other. If so, she'll be getting a good husband. I've known Ahmed for some time; he was at the Constabulary post near my camp, on Beta. It's too bad," he added, "that he seems to be getting nowhere on this Herckerd-Novaes investigation. It's certainly not from lack of trying."

"My police chief, Harry Steefer, is getting nowhere just as rapidly," Grego said. "He's ready to give the whole thing up, and when Harry Steefer gives up, it's hopeless."

"Do you think there is anything to this theory that somebody is training those Fuzzies to help catch other Fuzzies?"

Grego shook his head. "You know Fuzzies at least as well as I do, Governor. Almost two months; anything you can train a Fuzzy to do, you can train him to do it in less than that," he said. "And I don't see why anybody would try to catch wild Fuzzies, not with the bloodthirsty laws you've enacted. Criminals only take chances in proportion to profits, and almost anybody who wants a Fuzzy can get one free."

That was true. And there was no indication of any black market in Fuzzies here, and Jack's patrols over northern Beta Continent hadn't found any evidence that anybody was live-trapping Fuzzies there.

"Ahmed had an idea, for a while, that they were going into the export business; catching Fuzzies to smuggle out for sale off-planet."

"He mentioned that to Harry Steefer. Jack Holloway was talking to me about that, too; wanted to know what could be done to prevent it. I told him it would be impossible to get Fuzzies onto a ship from Darius, or onto Darius from Mallorysport Space Terminal. As long as we keep our 'flagrant and heinous space-traffic monopoly,' you can be sure no Fuzzies are going to be shipped off-planet."

"You think Ingermann really has anything to do with it?" he asked hopefully, recognizing the source of the quotation.

"If there is a black market in Fuzzies, Ingermann's back of it," Grego said, as though stating a natural law. "In the six or so years he's infected this planet, I've learned a lot about the *soi-disant* Honorable Hugo Ingermann, and none of it's been good."

"Ahmed Khadra thinks his attacks on the CZC space-monopoly may stem from a desire to get some way around your controls at the ground terminal here and on Darius. Of course, he's talking about a Government spaceport, and that would be just as tightly controlled . . ."

Grego hesitated for a moment, then dropped his cigarette to the ground and heeled it out. He leaned toward Rainsford in his chair.

"Governor, you know, yourself, that as things stand you can't build a second spaceport here," he said. "Ingermann knows that, too. He's making that issue to embarrass you and to attack the CZC at the same time. He has no expectation that your Government would build any spaceport facilities here. He certainly hopes not; he wants to do that himself."

"Where the devil would he get the money?"

"He could get it. Unless I miss my guess, he's getting

it now, or as soon as a ship can get in, on Marduk. There are a number of shipping companies who would like to get in here in competition with Terra-Baldur-Marduk Spacelines, and there are quite a few import-export houses there who would like to trade on Zarathustra in competition with CZC. Inside six months somebody will be trying to put in a spaceport here. If they can get land to set it on. And due to a great error in my judgment eight years ago, the land's available."

"Where?"

"Right here on Alpha Continent, less than a hundred miles from where we're sitting. A wonderful place for a spaceport. You weren't here, then, were you, Governor?"

"No. I came here, I blush to say, on the same ship that brought Ingermann, six and a half years ago."

"Well, you got here, and so did he, after it was over, but just before that we had a big immigration boom. At that time, the company wasn't interested in local business, just off-planet trade in veldbeest meat. A lot of independent concerns started, manufacturing, food-production, that sort of thing that we didn't want to bother with. We sold land north of the city, in mile and two-mile square blocks, about two thousand square miles of it. Then the immigrants stopped coming, and a lot of them moved away. There simply wasn't employment for them. Most of the companies that had been organized went broke. Some of the factories that were finished operated for a while; most of them were left unfinished. The banks took over some of the land; most of it got into the hands of the shylocks; and since the Fuzzy Trial Ingermann has been acquiring title to a lot of it. Since the Fuzzy Trial, nobody else has been spend-

ing money for real-estate; everybody expects to get all
the free land they want."

"Well, he'll probably make some money out of that,
but the people who come in here with the capital will
be the ones to control it, won't they?"

"Of course they will, but that's honest business; Ingermann isn't interested. He's expecting an increase of
about two to three hundred percent in the planetary
population in the next five years. With eighty percent
of the land-surface in public domain, that's probably an
under-estimate. Most of them will be voters; Ingermann's going to try to control that vote."

And if he did ... His own position was secure;
Colonial Governors were appointed, and it took something like the military intervention which had put him
into office to unseat one. But a Colonial Governor had
to govern through and with the consent of a Legislature.
He wasn't looking forward happily to a Legislature controlled by Hugo Ingermann. Neither, he knew, was
Grego.

He'd have to be careful, though. Grego wanted to
put the company back in its old pre-Fuzzy position of
planetary dominance. He was still violently opposed
to that.

It was almost dark, now. The Fuzzies had put the
final touches to the lacy trellis they had built, and came
crowding over, wanting Pappy Ben and Pappy Vic to
come look. They went and examined it, and spoke com-
mendation. Grego picked up Diamond; Flora and Fauna
were wanting him to go and sit down and furnish them
a lap to sit on.

"I've been worrying about just that," he said, when
he was back in his chair, with the Fuzzies climbing up
onto him. "A lot of the older planets are beginning to

overpopulate, and there's never room enough for every-body on Terra. There'll be a rush here in about a year. If I can only get things stabilized before then . . ."

Grego was silent for a moment. "If you're worried about all those public-health and welfare and service functions, forget about them for a while," he said. "I know, I said the company would discontinue them in ninety days, but that was right after the Pendarvis Decisions, and nobody knew what the situation was going to be. We can keep them going for a year, at least."

"The Government won't have any more money a year from now," he said. "And you'll expect compensation."

"Of course we will, but we won't demand gold or Federation notes. Tax-script, bonds, land-script . . ."

Land-script, of course; the law required a Colonial Government to make land available to Federation citizens, but it did not require such land to be given free. That might be one way to finance the Government.

It could also be a way for the Zarathustra Company, having gotten the Government deeply into debt, to regain what had been lost in the aftermath of the Fuzzy Trial.

"Suppose you have Gus Brannhard talk it over with Leslie Coombes," Grego was suggesting. "You can trust Gus not to stick the Government's foot into any bear-trap, can't you?"

"Why, of course, Mr. Grego. I want to thank you, very much, for this. That public services takeover was worrying me more than anything else."

Yet he couldn't feel relieved, and he couldn't feel grateful at all. He felt discomfited, and angry at himself more than at Grego.

XIX

GERD VAN RIEBEEK crouched at the edge of the low cliff, slowly twisting the selector-knob of a small screen in front of him. The view changed; this time he was looking through the eye of a pickup fifty feet below and five hundred yards to the left. Nothing in it moved except a wind-stirred branch that jiggled a spray of ragged leaves in the foreground. The only thing from the sound-outlet was a soft drone of insects, and the *tweet-twonk, tweet-twonk* of a presumably love-hungry banjo-bird. Then something just out of sight scuffled softly among the dead leaves. He turned up the sound-volume slightly.

"What do you think it is?"

Jack Holloway, beside him, rose to one knee, raising his binoculars.

"I can't see anything. Try the next one."

Gerd twisted the knob again. This pickup was closer the ground; it showed a vista of woods lit by shafts of sunlight falling between trees. Now he could hear rustling and scampering, and with ultrasonic earphone, Fuzzy voices:

"This way. Not far. Find *hatta-zosa*."

Jack was looking down at the open slope below the cliff.

"If that's what they call goofers, I see six of them from here," he said. "Probably a dozen more I can't see." He watched, listening. "Here they come, now."

The Fuzzies had stopped talking and were making very little noise; then they came into view; eight of them, in single file. The weapons they carried were longer and heavier than the prawn-killers of the southern Fuzzies, knobbed instead of paddle-shaped, and sharp-pointed on the other end. All of them had picked up stones which they carried in their free hands. They all stopped, then three of them backed away into the brush again. The other five spread out in a skirmish line and waited. He shut off the screen and crawled over beside Jack to peep over the edge of the cliff.

There were seven goofers, now; rodent-looking things with dark gray fur, a foot and a half long and six inches high at the shoulder, all industriously tearing off bark and digging at the roots of young trees. No wonder the woods were so thin, around here; if there were any number of them it was a wonder there were any trees at all. He picked up a camera and aimed it, getting some shots of them.

"Something else figuring on getting some lunch here," Jack said, sweeping the sky with his glasses. "Harpy, a couple of miles off. Ah, another one. We'll stick around a while; we may have to help our friends out."

The five Fuzzies at the edge of the brush stood waiting. The goofers hadn't heard them, and were still tearing and chewing at the bark and digging at the roots. Then, having circled around, the other three burst out suddenly, hurling their stones and running forward with their clubs. One stone hit a goofer and knocked it down;

instantly, one of the Fuzzies ran forward and brained it with his club. The other two rushed a second goofer, felling and dispatching it with their clubs. The other fled, into the skirmish line on the other side. Two were hit with stones, and finished off on the ground. The others got away. The eight Fuzzies gathered in a clump, seemed to debate pursuit for a moment, and then abandoned the idea. They had four goofers, a half-goofer apiece. That was a good meal for them.

They dragged their game together and began tearing the carcasses apart, using teeth and fingers, helping one another dismember them, tearing off skin and pulling meat loose, using stones to break bones. Gerd kept his camera going, filming the feast.

"Our gang's got better table-manners," he commented.

"Our gang have the knives we make for them. Beside, our gang mostly eat zatku, and they break off the manibles and make little lobster-picks out of them. They're ahead of our gang in one way, though. The Fuzzies south of the Divide don't hunt cooperatively," Jack said.

The two dots in the sky were larger and closer; a third had appeared.

"We better do something about that," he advised, reaching for his rifle.

"Yes." Jack put down the binoculars and secured his own rifle, checking it. "Let them eat as long as they can; they'll get a big surprise in a minute or so."

The Fuzzies seemed to be aware of the presence of the harpies. Maybe there were ultrasonic wing-vibration sounds they could hear; he couldn't be sure, even with the hearing aid. There was so much ultrasonic noise in the woods, and he hadn't learned, yet, to distinguish. The Fuzzies were eating more rapidly. Finally, one pointed and cried, *"Gotza bizzo!"* *Gotza* was another native zoological name he had learned, though the Fuzzies at Holloway's Camp mostly said, "Hah'py," now. The diners grabbed their weapons and what meat they could carry and dashed into the woods. One of the big pterodactyl-things was almost overhead, another was within a few hundred yards, and the third was coming in behind him. Jack sat up, put his left arm through his rifle-sling, cuddled the butt to his cheek and propped his elbows on his knees. The nearest harpy must have caught a movement in the brush below; it banked and started to dive. Jack's 9.7 magnum bellowed. The harpy made a graceless flop-over in the air and dropped. The one behind banked quickly and tried to gain altitude; Gerd shot it. Jack's rifle thundered again, and the third harpy thrashed leathery wings and dropped.

From below, there was silence, and then a clamor of Fuzzy voices:

"Harpies dead; what make do?"

"Thunder; maybe kill harpies! Maybe kill us next!"

"Bad place, this! *Bizzo, fazzu!*"

Roughly, *fazzu* meant, "Scram."

Jack was laughing. "Little Fuzzy took it a lot calmer the first time he saw me shoot a harpy," he said. "By that time, though, he'd seen so much he wasn't surprised at anything." He replaced the two fired rounds in the magazine of his rifle. "Well, *bizzo, fazzu;* we won't get any more movies around here."

They went around with the car, collecting the pick-ups they had planted, then lifted out, turning south toward the horizon-line of the Divide, the mountain range that stretched like the cross-stroke of an H between the West Coast Range and the Eastern Cordilleras. Evidently the Fuzzies never crossed it much; the language of the northern Fuzzies, while comprehensible, differed distinguishably from that spoken by the ones who had come in to the camp. Apparently the news of the bumper crop of zatku hadn't gotten up here at all.

They talked about that, cruising south at five thousand feet, with the foothills of the Divide sliding away under them and the line of sheer mountains drawing closer. They'd have to establish a permanent camp up here; contact these Fuzzies and make friends with them, give them tools and weapons, learn about them.

That was, if the Native Commission budget would permit. They talked about that, too.

Then they argued about whether to stay up here for another few days, or start back to the camp.

"I think we'd better go back," Jack said, somewhat regretfully. "We've been away for a week. I want to see what's going on, now."

"They'd screen us if anything was wrong."

"I know. I still think we'd better go back. Let's cross the Divide and camp somewhere on the other side, and go on in tomorrow morning."

"*Hokay; bizzo.*" He swung the aircar left a trifle. "We'll follow that river to the source and cross over there."

The river came down through a wide valley, narrowing and growing more rapid as they ascended it. Finally, they came to where it emerged, a white mountain torrent, from the mouth of a canyon that cut into the main range of the Divide. He took the car down to within a few hundred feet and cut speed, entering the canyon. At first, it was wide, with a sandy beach on either side of the stream and trees back to the mountain face and up the steep talus at the foot of it. Granite at the bottom, and then weathered sandstone, and then, for a couple of hundred feet, gray, almost unweathered flint.

"Gerd," Jack said, at length, "take her up a little, and get a little closer to the side of the canyon." He shifted in his seat, and got his binoculars. "I want a close look at that."

He wondered why, briefly. Then it struck him.

"You think that's what I think it is?" he asked.

"Yeah. Sunstone-flint." Jack didn't seem particularly happy about it. "See that little bench, about half way up? Set her down there. I'm going to take a look at that."

The bench, little more than a wide ledge, was covered with thin soil; a few small trees and sparse brush grew on it. A sheer face of gray flint rose for a hundred feet above it. They had no blasting explosives, but there was a microray scanner and a small vibrohammer in the toolkit. They set the aircar down and went to work, cracking and scanning flint, and after two hours they had a couple of sunstones. They were nothing spectacular—an irregular globe seven or eight millimeters in diameter and a small elipsoid not quite twice as big. However, when Jack held them against the hot bowl of his pipe, they began to glow.

"What are they worth, Jack?"

"I don't know. Some of these freelance gem-buyers would probably give as much as six or eight hundred for the big one. When the company still had the monopoly, they'd have paid about four-fifty. Be worth twenty-five hundred on Terra. But look around. This layer's three hundred feet thick; it runs all the way up the canyon, and probably for ten or fifteen miles along the mountain on either side." He knocked out his pipe, blew through the stem, and pocketed it. "And it all belongs to the Fuzzies."

He started to laugh at that, and then remembered. This was, by executive decree, the Fuzzy Reservation. The Fuzzies owned it and everything on it, and the Government and the Native Commission were only trustees. Then he began laughing again.

"But, Jack! The Fuzzies can't mine sunstones, and they wouldn't know what to do with them if they could."

"No. But this is their country. They were born here, and they have a right to live here, and beside that, we gave it to them, didn't we? It belongs to them, sunstones and all."

"But Jack..." He looked up and down the canyon at the gray flint on either side; as Jack said, it would extend for miles back into the mountain on either side. Even allowing one sunstone to ten cubic feet of flint, and even allowing for the enormous labor of digging them out... "You mean, just let a few Fuzzies scamper around over it and chase goofers, and not do anything with it?" The idea horrified him. "Why, they don't even know this is the Fuzzy Reservation."

"They know it's their home. Gerd, this has happened on other Class-IV planets we've moved in on. We give the natives a reservation; we tell them it'll be theirs forever, Terran's word of honor. Then we find something valuable on it—gold on Loki, platinum on Thor, vanadium and wolfram on Hathor, nitrates on Yggdrasil, uranium on Gimli. So the natives get shoved off onto another reservation, where there isn't anything anybody wants, and finally they just get shoved off, period. We aren't going to do that here, to the Fuzzies."

"What are you going to do? Try to keep it a secret?" he asked. "If that's what you want, we'll just throw those two sunstones in the river and forget about it," he agreed. "But how long do you think it'll be before somebody else finds out about it?"

"We can keep other people out of here. That's what the Fuzzy Reservation's for, isn't it?"

"We need people to keep people out; Paine's Marines, George Lunt's Protection Force. I think we can trust George. I wouldn't know about Paine. Anybody below them I wouldn't trust at all. Sooner or later somebody'll fly up this canyon and see this, and then it'll be out. And you know what'll happen then." He thought for a moment. "Are you going to tell Ben Rainsford?"

"I wish you hadn't asked me that, Gerd." Jack fumbled his pipe and tobacco out of his pocket. "I suppose I'll have to. Have to give him these stones; they're Government property. Well, *bizzo*; we'll go straight to camp." He looked up at the sun. "Make it in about three hours. Tomorrow I'll go to Mallorysport."

"I'm afraid to believe it, Dr. Jimenez," Ernst Mallin said. "It would be so wonderful if it were true. Can you be certain?"

"We're all certain, now, that this hormone, NFMp, is what prevents normal embryonic development," Juan Jimenez, in the screen, replied. "We're certain, now, that hokfusine combines destructively with NFMp; even Chris Hoenveld, he's seen it happen in a test tube, and he has to believe it whether he wants to or not. It appears that hokfusine also has an inhibitory effect on the glands secreting NFMp. But to be certain, we'll have to wait four more months, until the infants conceived after the mothers began eating Extee Three are born. Ideally, we should wait until the females we have begun giving daily doses of pure hokfusine conceive and bear children. But if I'm not certain now, I'm confident."

"What put your people onto this, Dr. Jimenez?"

"A hunch," the younger man smiled. "A hunch by the girl in Dr. Hoenveld's lab, Charlotte Tresca." The smile became an audible laugh. "Hoenveld is simply furious about it. No sound theoretical basis, just a lot of unsupported surmises. You know how he talks. He did have to grant her results; they've been duplicated. But he rejects her whole line of reasoning."

He would; Jan Christiaan Hoenveld's mind plodded obstinately along, step by step, from A to B to C to D; it wasn't fair for somebody suddenly to leap to W or X and run from there to Z. For his own part, Ernst Mallin respected hunches; he knew how much mental activity went on below the level of consciousness and with what seeming irrationality fragments of it rose to the conscious mind. His only regret was that he had so few good hunches, himself.

"Well, what was her reasoning?" he asked. "Or was it pure intuition?"

"Well, she just got the idea that hokfusine would neutralize the NFMp hormone, and worked from there," Jimenez said. "As she rationalizes it, all Fuzzies have a craving for land-prawn meat, without exception. This is a racial constant with them. Right?"

"Yes, as far as we can tell. I hate to use the word loosely, but I'd say, instinctual."

"And all Fuzzies, for which read, all studied individuals, have a craving for Extee Three. Once they taste the stuff, they eat it at every opportunity. This isn't a learned taste, like our taste for, say, coffee or tobacco or alcohol; every human has to learn to like all three. The Fuzzy's response to Extee Three is immediate and automatic. Still with it, Doctor?"

"Oh, yes; I've seen quite a few Fuzzies taking their

first taste of Extee Three. It's just what you call it;
a physical response." He gave that a moment's thought,
adding: "If it's an instinct, it's the result of natural
selection."

"Yes. She reasoned that a taste for the titanium-
molecule compound present both in land-prawns and
Extee Three contributed to racial survival; that Fuzzies
lacking it died out, and Fuzzies having it to a pronounced degree survived and transmitted it. So she went
to work—over Hoenveld's vehement objections that she
was wasting her time—and showed the effect of hokfusine on the NFMp hormone. Now, the physiologists
who had that theory about cyclic production of NFMp
getting out of phase with the menstrual cycle and per-
mitting an occasional viable birth are finding that the
NFMp fluctuations aren't cyclic at all but related to
hokfusine consumption."

"Well, you have a fine circumstantial case there.
Everything seems to fit together with everything else.
As you say, you'll have to wait about a year before
you can really prove a one-to-one relationship between
hokfusine and viable births, but if I were inclined to
gamble I'd risk a small wager on it."

Jimenez grinned. "I have, already, with Dr. Hoenveld.
I think it's money in the bank now."

Bennett Rainsford warmed the two sunstones between
his palms, then rolled them, like a pair of dice, on the
desk in front of him. He had been so happy, ever since
Victor Grego had called him to tell him what had been
discovered at Science Center about the hokfusine and
the NFMp hormone. They were on the right track, he
was sure of it, and in a few years all the Fuzzy children
would be born alive and normal.

And then, just after lunch, Jack Holloway had come dropping out of the sky from Beta Continent with this.

"You can't keep it a secret, Jack. You can't keep any discovery a secret, because anything anybody discovers, somebody else can, and will, discover later. Look how the power interests tried to suppress the discovery of direct conversion of nuclear energy to electric current, back in the First Century. Look how they tried to suppress the Abbot Drive."

"This is different," Jack Holloway argued, bullheadedly. "This isn't a scientific principle anybody, anywhere, can discover. This is something at a certain place, and if we can keep people away from it..."

"Quis custodiet ipsos custodes?" Then, realizing that Latin was *terra incognita* to Jack, he translated: "Who'll watch the watchmen?"

Jack nodded. "That's what Gerd said. A thing like that would be an awful strain on anybody's moral fiber. And you know what'll happen as soon as it gets out."

"There'd be pressure on me to open the Fuzzy Reservation. Hugo Ingermann's John Doe and Richard Roe and all. I suppose I could stall it off till a legislature was elected, but after that..."

"I wasn't talking about political pressure. I was talking about a sunstone rush. There'd be twenty thousand men stampeding up there, with everything they could put onto contragravity. And everything they could find to shoot with, too. And the longer it's stalled off, the worse it'll be, because in six months the off-planet immigrants'll start coming in."

He hadn't thought of that. He should have; he'd been on other frontier planets where rich deposits of mineral wealth had been discovered. And there was nothing in the Galaxy that concentrated more value in less bulk than sunstones.

"Ben, I've been thinking," Jack continued. "I don't like the idea, but it's the only idea I have. Those sunstones are in a little section about fifty miles square on the north side of the Divide. Suppose the Government makes that a sort of reservation-inside-the-reservation, and operates the sunstone mines. You do it before anything leaks out — announce that the Government has discovered sunstones on the Fuzzy Reservation, that the Government claims all the sunstones on Fuzzy land in the name of the Fuzzies, and that the Government is operating all sunstone mines, and it'll head off the rush, or the worst of it. And the Fuzzies'll get out of that immediate area; they won't stay around where there's underground blasting. And the money the Government gets out of it can go to the Fuzzies in protection and welfare and medical aid and *shoppo-diggo* and *shodda-bag* and *esteefee*."

"Have you any idea what it would cost to start an operation like that, before we could even begin getting out sunstones in paying quantities?"

"Yes. I've been digging sunstones as long as anybody knew there were sunstones. But this is a good thing, Ben, and if you have a good thing you can always finance it."

"It would protect the Fuzzies' rights, and they'd benefit enormously. But the initial expense..."

"Well, lease the mineral rights to somebody who could finance it. The Government would get a royalty, the Fuzzies would benefit, the Reservation would be kept intact."

"But who? Who would be able to lease it?"

He knew, even as he asked the question. The Charter-

194

less Zarathustra Company; they could operate that mine. Why, that mine would be something on the odd-jobs level, compared to what they'd done on the Big Blackwater Swamp. Lease them the entire mineral rights for the Reservation; that would keep everybody else out.

But it would put the Company back where they'd been before the Pendarvis Decisions; it would give them back their sunstone monopoly; it would . . . Why, it was unthinkable!

Unthinkable, hell. He was thinking about it now, wasn't he?

Victor Grego crushed out his cigarette and leaned back in his relaxer-chair, closing his eyes. From the Fuzzyroom, he could hear muted voices, and the frequent popping of shots. Diamond was enjoying a screen-play. He was very good about keeping the volume turned down, so as not to bother Pappy Vic, but he'd get some weird ideas about life among the Hagga from some of those shows. Well, the good Hagga always licked the bad Hagga in the end, that was one thing.

He went back to thinking about bad Hagga, four of them in particular. Ivan Bowlby, Spike Heenan, Raul Laporte, Leo Thaxter.

Mallorysport was full of bad Hagga, on the lower echelons, but those four were the General Staff. Bowlby was the entertainment business. Beside the telecast show which Diamond was watching at the moment, that included prize-fights, nightclubs, prostitution and, without doubt, dope. Maybe he'd like to get Fuzzies as attractions at his night-spots, and through that part of his business he could make contacts with well to do people who wanted Fuzzies, couldn't adopt them, and would pay fancy prices for them. If there really were a black market, he'd be in it.

Spike Heenan was gambling; crap-games, numbers racket, bookmaking. On sport-betting, his lines and Bowlby's would cross with mutual profit. Laporte was racketeering, extortion, plain old-fashioned country-style crime. And stolen goods, of course, and, while there'd been money in it, illicit gem-buying.

Leo Thaxter was the biggest, and the most respectably fronted, of the four. L. Thaxter, Loan Broker & Private Financier. He loaned money publicly at a righteously legal seven percent; he also loaned, at much higher rates, to all the shylocks in town, who, in turn, loaned it at six-for-five to people who could not borrow elsewhere, including suckers who went broke in Spike Heenan's crap-games, and he used Raul Laporte's hoodlums to do his collecting.

And, notoriously but unprovably, behind them stood Hugo Ingermann, Mallorysport's unconvicted underworld generalissimo.

Maybe they were just before proving it, now. Leslie Coombes' investigators had established that all four of them, and especially Thaxter, were the dummy owners behind whom Ingermann controlled most of the land the company had unwisely sold eight years ago, the section north of Mallorysport that was now dotted with abandoned factories and commercial buildings. And it was pretty well established that those four had been the John Doe, Richard Roe, *et alii,* who had been represented in court by Ingermann just after the Pendarvis Decisions.

Strains of music were now coming from the Fuzzyroom; the melodrama was evidently over. He opened his eyes, lit another cigarette, and began going over what he knew about Ingermann's four chief henchmen. Thaxter; he'd come to Zarathustra a few years before Ingermann. Small-time racketeer, at first, and then he'd tried to organize labor unions, but labor unions organized by outsiders had been frowned upon by the company, and he'd been shown the wisdom of stopping that. Then he'd organized an independent planters' marketing cooperative, and from that he'd gotten into shylocking. There'd been some woman with him, at first, wife or reasonable facsimile. Maybe she was still around; have Coombes look into that. She might be willing to talk.

Diamond strolled in from the Fuzzy-room.

"Pappy Vic! Make talk with Diamond, *plis*."

Lieutenant Fitz Mortlake, acting-in-charge of company detective bureau for the 1800-2400 shift, yawned. Twenty more minutes; less than that if Bert Eggers got in early to relieve him. He riffled through the stack of complaint-sheet copies on the desk and put a paperweight on them. In the squadroom outside the mechanical noises of card-machines and teleprinters and the occasional howl of a sixty-speed audiovisual transmission were being replaced by human sounds, voices and laughter and the scraping of chairs, as the midnight-to-six shift began filtering in. He was wondering whether to go home and read till he became sleepy, or drift around the bars to see if he could pick up a girl, when Bert Eggers pushed past a couple of sergeants at the door and entered.

"Hi, Fitz; how's it going?"

"Oh, quiet. We found out where Jayser hid that stuff; we have all of it, now. And Millman and Nogahara caught those kids who were stealing engine parts out of

Warehouse Ten. We have them in detention; we haven't questioned them yet."

"We'll take care of that. They work for the company?"

"Two of them do. The third is just a kid, seventeen. Juvenile Court can have him. We think they were selling the stuff to Honest Hymie."

"Uhuh. I'll suspect anybody they all call Honest Anybody or anything," Eggers said, sitting down as he vacated the chair.

He took off his coat, pulled his shoulder holster and pistol from the bottom drawer and put it on, resuming the coat. He gathered up his lighter and tobacco pouch, and then discovered that his pipe was missing, and hunted the desk-top for it, unearthing it from under some teleprinted photographs.

"What are these?" Eggers asked, looking at them.

"Herckerd and Novaes, false alarm number steen thousand. A couple of woods-tramps who turned up on Epsilon."

Eggers made a sour face. "Those damn Fuzzies have made more work for us," he began. "And now, my kids are after me to get them one. So's my wife. You know what? Fuzzies are a status-symbol, now. If you don't have a Fuzzy, you might as well move to Junktown with the rest of the bums."

"I don't have a Fuzzy, and I haven't moved to Junktown yet."

"You don't have kids in high school."

"No, thank God!"

"Bet he doesn't have finance-company trouble, either," one of the sergeants in the doorway said.

Bert was going to make some retort to that. Before he could, another voice spoke up:

"Yeeek!"

"Speak of the devil," somebody said.

"You have that Fuzzy in here, Fitz?" Eggers demanded. "Where the hell . . . ?"

"There he is," one of the men in the doorway said, pointing.

The Fuzzy, who had been behind the desk-chair, came out into view. He pulled the bottom of Eggers' coat, yeeking again. He looked like a hunchback Fuzzy.

"What's he got on his back?" Eggers reached down. "Whatta you got there, anyhow?"

It was a little rucksack, with leather shoulder-straps and a drawstring top. As soon as Eggers displayed an interest in it, the Fuzzy climbed out of it as though glad to be rid of it. Mortlake picked it up and put it on the desk; over ten pounds, must weigh almost as much as the Fuzzy. Eggers opened the drawstrings and put his hand into it.

"It's full of gravel," he said, and brought out a handful.

The gravel was glowing faintly. Eggers let go of it as though it were as hot as it looked.

"Holy God!" It was the first time he ever heard anybody screaming in baritone. "The damn things are *sunstones!*"

XX

"But what for?" Diamond was insisting. "What for Big Ones first, *bang, bang,* make dead? Not good. What for not make friend, make help, have fun?"

"Well, some Big Ones bad, make trouble. Other Big Ones fight to stop trouble."

"But what for Big Ones be bad? Why not everybody make friend, have fun, make help, be good?"

Now how in Nifflheim could you answer a question like that? Maybe that was what Ernst Mallin meant when he said Fuzzies were the sanest people he'd ever seen. Maybe they were too sane to be bad, and how could a non-sane human explain to them?

"Pappy Vic not know. Maybe Unka Ernst, Unka Panko, know."

The bell of the private communication screen began its slow tolling. Diamond looked around; this was something that didn't happen often. He rose, taking Diamond from his lap and setting him on the chair, then went to the wall and put the screen on. It was Captain Morgan Lansky, at Chief Steefer's desk. He looked as though a planetbuster had just dropped in front of him and hadn't exploded yet.

"Mr. Grego; the gem-vault! Fuzzies in it, robbing it!"

He conquered the impulse to ask Lansky if he were drunk or crazy. Lansky was neither; he was just frightened.

"Take it easy, Morgan. Tell me about it. First, what you know's happened, and then what you think is happening."

"Yes, sir." Lansky got hold of himself; for an instant he was silent. "Ten minutes ago, in the captain's office at detective bureau; the shifts were changing, and both lieutenants were there. A Fuzzy came out of a storeroom in back of the office; he had a little knapsack on his back, with about twelve pounds of sunstones in it. The Fuzzy's here now, so are the sunstones. Do you want to see them?"

"Later; go ahead." Then, before Lansky could speak, he asked: "Sure he came out of this storeroom?"

"Yes, sir. There was five-six men in the doorway to the squadroom, he couldn't of come through that way. And the only way he could of got into this storeroom was out a ventilation duct there. The grating over it was open."

"That sounds reasonable. He could have gotten into the gem-vault through the ventilation system too."

The entrance to the gem-vault stairway was on the same floor as the detective bureau. The inlet and outlet screens were hinged, and the latch worked from either side to allow any outlet-screen to be put on anywhere. And the sunstones couldn't have come from anywhere else; just yesterday he'd had to go down and let Evins in to put away what had accumulated in his office safe.

"Ten minutes; what's been done since?"

"Carlos Hurtado's here, he hadn't gone home. He's staying, and so are most of the pre-midnight men. We put out a quiet alert to all the police in the building. We're blocking off everything from the top of the fourteenth level down, and a second block around the fifteenth. I called the Chief; he's coming in. Hurtado's calling the Constabulary and the Mallorysport police for men and vehicles to blockade the building from the outside. I've sent calls out for Dr. Mallin, and for Mr. E. Evins, and I've sent out for as many hearing-aids as I can get."

"That was good. Now, have a jeep or something up here for me right away; I'll have to open the gem-vault. And have men there to meet me. With sono-stunners; there may be more Fuzzies inside. And get hold of the building superintendent and the ventilation engineer, and get plans of the ventilation system."

"Right. Anything else, Mr. Grego?"

"Not that I can think of now. Be seeing you."

He blanked the screen. Diamond, in the chair, was looking at him wide-eyed.

"Pappy Vic; what make do?"

He looked at Diamond for a moment. "Diamond, you remember when bad Big Ones bring you, other Fuzzies, here?" he asked. "You know other Fuzzies again, you see them?"

"*Yeh, tsure.* Good friend; know again."

"*Hokay.* Stay put; Pappy Vic be back."

He ran into the kitchenette and gathered a couple of tins of Extee Three. Returning, he found a hearing-aid—Diamond was using his Fuzzyphone, and he hadn't needed it—and pocketed it. Then, swinging Diamond to his shoulder, he went outside. Just as he emerged onto the terrace, a silver-trimmed maroon company airjeep, lettered POLICE, lifted above the edge of the terrace, turned, and glided down. He thought, again, that police vehicles should have some distinctive color-scheme to distinguish them from ordinary company cars. Talk about that with Harry Steefer, some time. Then the jeep was down and the pilot had opened the door. He climbed in and held Diamond on his lap, while the pilot reported him aboard. Then he took the radio handphone himself.

"Grego; who's there?" he asked.

"Hurtado. We have everything from the fourteenth level down to the sixteenth sealed off, inside and out. Captain Lansky and Lieutenant Eggers have gone to meet you at the gem-vault. Dr. Mallin's coming in; so's Miss Glenn and Captain Khadra of the ZNPF. Maybe they can get something out of this Fuzzy." He muttered something bitterly. "Questioning Fuzzies; what's police work coming to next?"

"Teaching Fuzzies to crack safes; what's crime coming to next? You get the ventilation-system plans yet?"

"They're coming up; so's the ventilation engineer. You think there's more Fuzzies than this one?"

"Four more. And two men, named Phil Novaes and Moses Herckerd."

Hurtado was silent for a moment, then cursed. "Now why in Nifflheim didn't I think of that?" he demanded. "Sure!"

They went inside from a landing-stage on the third level down. There were police there, with portable machine guns, and a couple of cars. Work was going on in some of the offices along the horizontal vehicle-way, but no excitement. They encountered a police car in the vertical shaft just above the fourteenth level down; the jeep pilot put on his red-and-white blinker and picked up the handphone of his loudspeaker, saying,

"Mr. Grego here; please don't delay us." The car moved out of the way.

The fifteenth level down was police country. Everything was superficially quiet, but a number of vehicles were concentrated around the horizontal ways from the vertical shaft. The pilot set the jeep down at the entrance to the gem-buyer's offices. Morgan Lansky and a detective were waiting there. He got out, holding Diamond, and the pilot handed the tins of Extee Three to the detective. Lansky, who seemed to have recovered his aplomb, grinned.

"Interpreter, Mr. Grego?" he asked.

"Yes, and maybe he can make identification. I think he knows these Fuzzies."

It took Lansky two seconds to get that. Then he nodded.

"Sure. That would explain everything."

They went through the door, and, inside, it was immediately evident that the security-regulation book had gone out the airlock. The portcullis was raised, though a couple of submachine-gunners loitered watchfully in front of it. Half a dozen men, all carrying sono-stunners, short carbines with flaring muzzles like ancient blunderbusses, fell in behind them. The door at the end of the short hall was open, too, and nobody was bothering with identity-checks.

Nobody was supposed to be within sight of him when he opened the vault, but he ignored that, too. Lansky, Eggers, the man who was carrying the two tins of Extee Three, and the men with the stunners all crowded down the stairway after him. Quickly he punched the nonsense sentence out on the keyboard. Ten seconds later the door receded and slid aside.

Inside, the lights were on, as always; bright as they

were, they could not dim the many-colored glow on the black velvet table-top, where two Fuzzies were playing concentratedly with a thousand or so sunstones. A little rope ladder, just big enough for a Fuzzy, dangled past the light-shade from the air-outlet above.

Both Fuzzies looked up, startled. One said in accusing complaint, "You not say stones make shine; you say just stones, like always." His companion looked at them for a moment, and then cried: "Not know these Big Ones! How come this place?"

Lansky, who had been holding Diamond while he had been using the keyboard, followed him in. Diamond saw the two on the table and jabbered in excited recognition. He took Diamond and set him on the table with the others.

"Not be afraid," he said. "I not hurt. He friend; show him pretty things."

Recognition was mutual; the other Fuzzies were hugging Diamond and talking rapidly. Lansky had gone to a communication screen and was punching a call-number.

"You get away from bad Big Ones, too?" Diamond was asking. "How you come this place?"

"Big Ones bring us. Make us go through long little hole. Tell us, get stones, like at other place."

What other place, he wondered. The other strange Fuzzy was saying:

"All-time, Big Ones make us go through long little holes, get stones. We get stones, Big Ones give us good things to eat. Not get stones, Big Ones angry. Make hurt, put us in dark place, not give anything to eat, make us do again."

"Who has the Extee Three?" he asked. "Open a tin for me."

"*Esteefee!*" Diamond, hearing him, repeated. "Pappy Vic give *esteefee; hoksu-fusso.*"

Lansky had Hurtado in the screen; he was standing aside to allow the latter to see what was going on in the gem-vault. Hurtado was swearing.

"Now, we gotta make everything in the building Fuzzy-proof," he was saying. "The Chief's just come in." He turned. "Hey, Chief, come and look at this!"

Eggers had the Extee Three; he got the tin open. Taking the cake from him, he broke it in three, then shoved a couple of million sols in sunstones out of the way and gave a piece to each of the Fuzzies. The two little jewel-thieves knew just what it was, and began eating at once. Telling Eggers to keep an eye on them, he went to the screen. In it, Harry Steefer was cursing even more fluently than Hurtado. He broke off and greeted:

"Hello, Mr. Grego. Beside what's on the table, are there any sunstones left?"

"I haven't checked, yet."

He looked around. All the drawers had been pulled out of the cabinet; the Fuzzies had evidently gotten at the upper rows by stacking and standing on the ones from below. Lansky was examining a couple of small canvas rucksacks he had found.

"What's it look like, Captain?"

"Don't come around the table, anybody," Lansky warned. "The floor's all over stones, here."

"Then we have some left. Has Conrad Evins come in, yet?"

"We're still trying to contact him," Steefer said. "Dr. Mallin's here, and Captain Khadra and Miss Glenn are on the way here. I'm going over to operation-command room, now; I'll leave somebody here."

"Suppose you leave the Fuzzy in your office, too. I'll

bring this pair up, and Diamond can help question them all."

Steefer assented, then excused himself to talk to somebody in the room with him. One of the detectives, who had gone out, returned with a broom and dustpan; he held the pan while Lansky swept the scattered sunstones up. There were more than he had expected, perhaps as many as half of them. He poured them into drawers, regardless of size or grade; they could be sorted out later. All the Fuzzies protested strenuously when he began gathering up the ones on the table; even Diamond wanted to play with them. He consoled them with the other cake of Extee Three, and assured Diamond, who assured his friends, that Pappy Vic would provide other pretties.

"Captain, you and Lieutenant Eggers and a couple of men stay here," he said. "I think we have two more Fuzzies, and they may be back for more stones. Catch them by hand if you can, stun them if you have to. Try not to hurt them, but get them, and bring them to the Chief's office. That's where I'm going now."

"Christ, I wish they'd hurry! What do you think's keeping them?"

That was the tenth or twelfth time Phil Novaes had said that in the last twenty minutes. Phil was getting on edge. Been on edge ever since they'd come here, and getting edgier every minute. Moses Herckerd was beginning to worry just a little about that. Losing your nerve was the surest way to disaster in a spot like this, and it would be disaster to both of them. Phil had been a little overconfident, at the beginning; that had been bad, too.

Getting the car hidden, on the unoccupied ninth level

down, had been easy enough; they'd stowed it in one of the unfinished main office rooms close to where they'd kept the Fuzzies, two months ago. He knew the company police had started patroling the unoccupied levels after that one damned Fuzzy had gotten away from them and, of all places, into Victor Grego's own apartment. Still, the place where they'd left the car was safe enough.

The long descent, nearly a thousand feet, among the water mains and ventilation mains to the fifteenth level down, had been hard and dangerous, clinging to the contragravity lifter with the Fuzzies jostling about in the box. Once this was over, he hoped he'd never see another damned Fuzzy as long as he lived. Phil had been all right then; he'd had to keep his mind on what he was doing, keep the lifter from swinging out and carrying them away from the hand-holds. It had been after they had gotten onto this ledge at the ventilation-duct outlet that Phil's nerves had begun to get away from him.

"Take it easy, Phil," he whispered. "They have half a mile, coming and going, through those ducts. And they have to fill their packs in the vault, and they always poke around doing that. Never can teach the buggers to hurry."

"Well, something could have happened. Maybe they took a wrong turn and got lost. That place is a lot more complicated than the practice setup."

"Oh, they'll get out all right. They all made three trips already without anything going wrong, didn't they?" he said. "And don't talk so damned loud."

That was what he was worried about, as much as anything. The whole company police force was concentrated around the place where he and Novaes were waiting. They were outside the actual police zone, but all the

other emergency services—fire protection, radiation safe-
ty, the first-aid dispensaries and the ambulance hangars
—were all around them, and sound carried an incredible
distance through these shafts and air ducts and conduits.

"We have enough, now," Phil said. "Let's just pick up
and go, now. Why, we must have fifty million already."

"But out and leave the Fuzzies?"

"Hell with the Fuzzies," Phil said.

"Hell with the Fuzzies, hell! Haven't you found out
yet that Fuzzies can talk. We've spent two months, now,
cooped up indoors, because that Fuzzy Grego found put
the finger on us. We've got to get all five back, and
we've got to finish them off. If we don't and the police
get hold of them, they'll finish us."

Phil, who was stooping by the rectangular outlet,
looked up.

"I hear something. A couple of them, talking."

He turned on his hearing-aid and put his head to the
opening beside Phil's. Yes, a couple of Fuzzies talking;
arguing about how far it was yet.

"As soon as they come out, let's just shove them into
the chute," Phil argued, nodding toward the access-port
to the trash-chute, that went seven hundred feet down
to the mass-energy converters.

That was where the Fuzzies would go, all of them,
when the sunstones were all out of the vault. But the
sunstones weren't all out. He doubted if they had more
than half of them, yet.

"No, not yet. Here they come; grab the first one."

Novaes caught the Fuzzy as he came out. He caught
the second. They were both carrying loaded packs. He
slipped the straps down over the Fuzzy's arms and gave
him to Novaes to hold, then loosened the drawstrings,
emptying the stones into the open suitcase along with

the other gems. Then he put the rucksack onto the Fuzzy's back.

"All right. In with you. Go get stones."

The Fuzzy said something, he wasn't sure what, in a complaining tone. *Fusso;* that meant food, or eat. Important word to a Fuzzy.

"No. You get stone; then I give *fusso.* He shoved the Fuzzy back into the ventilation duct. "Let's unload yours and send him back. As long as there's sunstones in there, we want them."

A uniformed sergeant was holding down Chief Steefer's desk, smoking what was probably one of the Chief's cigars and talking to a girl in another screen. Across the room, Ernst Mallin, Ahmed Khadra and Sandra Glenn were talking to a Fuzzy who sat on the edge of a table, contentedly munching Extee Three. Khadra was in evening clothes, and Sandra was wearing something glamorous with a lot of black lace. She was also wearing a sunstone which he hadn't noticed before, on the third finger of her left hand. *Wanted, Fuzzy Sitter. Apply Victor Grego.*

They set Diamond and his friends on the floor; he thanked and dismissed the men who had helped him with them. As soon as they saw the Fuzzy on the table, they raised an outcry and ran forward; the Fuzzy on the table dropped to the floor and hurried to meet them.

"What did you get from him?" he asked.

"Herckerd and Novaes, natch," Khadra said, disgustedly. "All the time I was looking for a black market that wasn't there, they were right here in town somewhere, being taught to steal sunstones. Fagin-racket, by God!"

"Herckerd and Novaes and who else?"

"Two other men, and one woman. And just the five Fuzzies Herckerd and Novaes brought in along with Diamond. They were somewhere not more than fifteen minutes by air from Company House all the time. This gang taught them to go through ventilator ducts, and open the screen-covers on the inlets, and use rope ladders and get stones out of cabinets. They must have had a mockup of the gem-vault and the ventilation system. They had to practice all the time. If they cleaned out the cabinets and brought the stones, river-gravel, I suppose, out, they got Extee Three. If they goofed, they were punished, electric shock, I suppose, and shoved in a dungeon with nothing to eat. You know, they could be shot for that."

"They oughtn't to be shot; they ought to be burned at the stake!" Sandra cried angrily.

Gentler sex, indeed! "Well, I'll settle for shooting, if we can catch them. Done anything in aid of that yet?"

"Not too much," Mallin regretted. "His vocabulary is limited, and he hasn't words for much that he experienced. "We've been trying to learn his route through the ventilation system. He knows how he went in to the gem-vault, but he simply can't verbalize it."

"Diamond; you help Pappy Vic. Make talk for Unka Ernst, Unka Ahmed, Auntie Sandra; help other Fuzzies make talk about bad Big Ones, about place where were, about what make do, about how go through long little holes." He turned to Khadra. "Has he seen Herckerd and Novaes on screen?"

"Not yet; we've just been talking to him, so far."

"Better let all three of them see those audiovisuals; get identifications made. And keep on about the ventilation ducts. See if any of them can tell which way they went toward the gem-vault, and what kind of a place they went in at."

XXI

CROSSING THE hall, he found the operation-command room busy, in a quiet and almost leisurely manner. Everybody knew what to do, and was getting it done with a minimum of fuss. A group of men, policemen and engineers, were huddled at a big table, going over plans, on big sheets and on photoprint screens. More men, police and maintenance people, gathered around a big solidigraph model of the fourteeth, fifteenth and sixteenth levels, projected in a tri-di screen. The thing was transparent, and looked almost anatomical; well, Company House was an organism of a sort. Respiratory system; the ventilation, in which everybody was interested. Circulatory system; the water-lines. Excretory system; sewage disposal.

And now it had been invaded by a couple of inimical microbes, named Phil Novaes and Moses Herckerd, whom the police leucocytes were seeking to neutralize.

He looked at it for a while, then strolled on to the banks of viewscreens. Views of halls and vehicle-ways, mostly empty, patrolled here and there by police or hastily mobilized and armed maintenance workers. Views of landing-stages, occupied by police and observed from aircars. A view from a car a thousand feet over the building, in which a few Constabulary and city police vehicles circled slowly, blockading the building from outside. He nodded in satisfaction; they couldn't get out of the building, and as soon as enough of the fifty-odd widely scattered locations from which they might be operating could be eliminated, the police would close in on them.

In one screen from a pickup installed over the door in the gem-vault, he could see Morgan Lansky, Bert Eggers and two detectives, coatless and perspiring, around the electrically warmed table-top, staring at the little rope ladder that dangled down around the light-shade. In another screen, from a high pickup in a corner of Harry Steefer's office, the uniformed sergeant at the desk watched Ernst Mallin and Ahmed Khadra fussing with a screen, while Sandra Glenn sat on the floor talking to Diamond and his three friends.

Harry Steefer sat alone at the command-desk, keeping track of everything at once. He went over and sat down beside him.

"Mr. Grego. We don't seem to be making too much progress," the Chief said. "Everything's secure so far, though."

"Have the news services gotten hold of it yet?"

"I don't believe. Planetwide News called the city police to find out what all the cars were doing around Company House; somebody told them that it was a shipment of valuables being taken under guard to the space terminal. They seemed to accept that."

"We can't sit on it indefinitely."

"I hope we can till we catch these people."

"Have you contacted Conrad Evins yet?"

"No. He's not at home; here, I'll show you."

Steefer punched out a call on one of his communication screens. When it lighted, the chief gem-buyer's wide-browed, narrow chinned face looked out of it.

"This is a recording, made at 2100, Conrad Evins speaking. Mrs. Evins and I are going out; we will not be home until after midnight," Evins' voice said. Then the screen flickered, and the recording began again.

"I could put out an emergency call for him, but I don't want to," Steefer said. "We don't know how many people outside the building are involved in this, and we don't want to alarm them."

"No. Four men and one woman; the Fuzzies say there were only two men, presumably Herckerd and Novaes, brought them here. That means two men and a woman somewhere outside waiting for them. And we don't really need Evins, at present. It's after midnight now; we can keep calling at his home."

Evins and his wife had probably gone to a show, or visiting. Evins' wife; he couldn't seem to recall ever having met her. He'd heard something or other about her . . . He shoved that aside.

"Don't they have little robo-snoopers they use to go through the ventilation ducts?" he asked.

"Yes. Mr. Guerrin, the ventilation engineer, has a dozen of them. He suggested using them, but I vetoed it till I could see what you thought. Those things float on contragravity, and even a miniature Abbot drive generator makes quite an ultrasonic noise. We still have two Fuzzies loose in the ventilation system; we don't want to scare them, do we?"

"No. Let them carry on. There's a chance they may come out in the gem-vault, if we don't frighten them."

He looked across the room at the view-screens. Khadra and Mallin had their screen set up, Sandra had brought the Fuzzies over in front of it, and Diamond seemed to be explaining about view-screens and audiovisual screens to the others. In the gem-vault screen, Lansky and the others were leaning forward across the table, listening. They had a couple of hearing-aids, now, which Eggers and one of his detectives were using. Lansky turned to make frantic gestures at the pickup. Steefer picked up a speaker-phone and advised everybody to pay attention to the gem-vault screen.

For one of those ten-second eternities, nothing happened in the screen. A moment later, a Fuzzy came climbing down the ladder. One of the detectives would have grabbed him; Eggers stopped him. A moment later, another Fuzzy appeared.

Eggers caught him by the feet with both hands and pulled him off the ladder; the Fuzzy hit Eggers in the face with his fist. The first Fuzzy, having dropped to the table, tried to get up the ladder again; Lansky grabbed him. One of the detectives came to Egger's assistance. Then the struggle was over, and the two prisoners had been secured. Lansky was yelling:

"We got them both! We're bringing them up."

Steefer yelled to the girl who was monitoring the screen to cut in sound transmission and tell Lansky and one man to remain on guard; Lansky acknowledged, and Eggers and one of the detectives left the vault, each carrying a Fuzzy. In the screen from Steefer's office, they had an audiovisual of Moses Herckerd on the screen; it was the employment interview film, and Herckerd was talking about his educational background and former job experience. Steefer was talking to the sergeant at his desk; the latter beckoned Ahmed Khadra over.

"Good," Khadra said, when Steefer told him what had happened. "That's all of them. We'll run Herckerd over for them when they come up, and show them Novaes.

216

They're the two who brought them here tonight, the three we have here all say so."

"They're still in here," Steefer said. "That leaves two men and a woman outside. I wonder . . ."

"I think I know who they are, Chief."

It was just a guess, of course, but it fitted. He had suddenly remembered what he knew about Mrs. Conrad Evins.

When Leo Thaxter, now Loan Broker & Private Financier, first came to Zarathustra ten years ago, a woman had come with him, but she hadn't been a wife or reasonable facsimile, she had been a sister or reasonable facsimile. Rose Thaxter. After a while, she had left Thaxter and married a company minerologist named Conrad Evins, who, after the discovery of the sunstones, had become chief company gem-buyer.

"What's that call-number of Evins'?" he asked Steefer, and when Steefer gave it, he repeated it to Khadra. "When those other Fuzzies come in, call it. It'll be answered by an audiovisual recording. See if the kids recognize him."

Steefer looked at him, more amused than surprised. "I wouldn't have thought of that, myself, Mr. Grego. It seems to fit, though."

"Hunch." If anybody respected hunches, it would be a cop. "I just remembered who Evins was married to. Rose Thaxter."

"*Yeh!*" Steefer muttered something else. "I know that, too; I just never connected it. It all hangs together, too."

For a couple of minutes, they were both talking at the same time, telling one another just how it did hang together, and watching the screen from Steefer's office. Eggers and the detective were coming in, still coatless, carrying a Fuzzy apiece; the one Eggers was carrying was trying to get the gun out of the lieutenant's shoulder-holster.

Of course it hung together. Somebody in the gang had to have exact knowledge of the layout of the gem-vault, which Evins, and very few others, could provide. The arrangement of the ventilation-ducts wasn't classified top-secret; anybody in Evins' position could have gotten that. They had to have a place to keep the Fuzzies, big enough to build a replica of the gem-vault and of the ventilation system. Well, there were all those vacant factories and warehouses out in the district everybody called Mortgageville. The ones Hugo Ingermann had been acquiring title to, with Thaxter as dummy buyer. How Herckerd and Novaes had been roped in wasn't immediately important; catch them and question them and that would emerge. Ten to one, Rose Thaxter, Mrs. Conrad Evins, was the connecting-link and mainspring.

The Fuzzies in Steefer's office were having a reunion. Khadra and Mallin and Sandra were trying to get them to look at the communication-screen. He turned to Steefer.

"Get some men to Conrad Evins' place; make a thorough search, for anything that might look like evidence of anything."

"They won't be there."

"No. They'll be in one of those buildings over in Mortgageville, and we don't know which one. I'm going to call Ian Ferguson."

He told Ferguson quickly what he suspected. The Constabulary commandant nodded.

"Reasonable," he agreed. "I'll call the city police for help; we'll close the place off so nobody can get in or out and then we'll start making a search. It's only about two thousand square miles, and there are only about three hundred buildings on it," he added. "I think I'll call Casagra, too, and see how many Marines he can give me."

"Well, take your time searching; just make sure anybody who's there now stays there. We'll give you what help we can as soon as we can."

He looked up at the screen from Steefer's office. Khadra had called Evins' home, now, and he could hear Evins' recorded voice stating that he wouldn't be home before midnight. The Fuzzies evidently recognized him. It was also evident that they didn't like him.

"And put out a general alert to pick up Evins, Mrs. Evins, and Leo Thaxter, and I don't think you need to worry about how much noise you make doing it."

"And Ivan Bowlby, and Raul Laporte, and Spike Heenan," Ferguson added. "And any or all of their hoods." He thought for a moment. "And Hugo Ingermann. We may finally have grounds for interrogating him as a suspect. I'll call Gus Brannhard, too."

"And Leslie Coombes; he'll be a help."

"All right, everybody!" Steefer was calling out with his loudspeaker. "We have all the Fuzzies out; now let's get the show started!" Then he rose and went around the desk.

Khadra was on the communication screen from the Chief's desk:

"They made that fellow Evins, all right. He was one of the gang. Who is he?"

"Well, he used to be the Company's chief gem-buyer, up to fifteen minutes ago, but now he has been discharged, without notice, severance-pay or recommendation." He thought for a moment. "Captain, are those Fuzzies' feet dirty?" he asked.

"Huh?" Khadra started at him for an instant, then nodded. "Yes, they are; gray-brown dust. Same kind of dust on their fur."

"Uhuh; that's good." He rose and went to the big table and the solidigraph, where Steefer was already talking to a dozen or so men. He saw Niles Guerrin, the ventilation engineer, and pulled him aside.

"Niles, the insides of those ducts are dusty?" he asked.

"The ones that carry stale air to the reconditioners," Guerrin replied. "Dust from the air in the rooms . . ."

"They're the ones we're interested in. Now, these snoopers, robo-inspectors; could they pick up tracks the Fuzzies make, or traces where they've brushed against the sides of the ducts?"

"Yes, sure. They have a full optical reception and transmission system for visible light and infra-red light, and controllable magnifying vision . . ."

"How soon can you get them started, from the gem-vault and from the captain's office in detective head-quarters?"

"Right away; we've set up screens and controls for them in here; did that right at the start."

"Good." He raised his voice. "Chief! Captain Hurtado, Lieutenant Mortlake; *do-bizzo*. We're going to fill the ventilation system with snoopers, now."

Phil Novaes looked at his watch. It was still 0130, the damned thing must have stopped, and he was sure he'd wound it. Holding his wrist to catch the dim light from above he squinted at the second-hand. It was still making its slow circuit around the dial. It must have been only a few seconds since he had looked at it last.

"Herk, let's get the hell out of here," he urged. "They

aren't coming out at all. It's been an hour since the last two went in."

"Thirty-five minutes," Herckerd said.

"Well, it's been over an hour since the other three went in. Something's gone wrong; we'll wait here till hell freezes over . . ."

"We'll wait here a little longer, Phil. We still have fifty million in sunstones to wait for, and we want to get those Fuzzies and shut them up for good."

"We have better than fifty million already. All we'll get'll be a hole in the head if we stay around here any longer. I know what's happened, those Fuzzies have gone out some other way; they're running around loose, packing sunstones . . ."

"Be quiet, Phil." Herckerd reached to his shirt pocket to turn on his hearing-aid and put his head to the ventilation duct opening. "I hear something in there." He snapped off the hearing-aid, listened, and snapped it on again. "It's ultrasonic, whatever it is. Probably vibration in the walls of the duct. Now just take it easy, Phil. Nobody knows there's anything happening at all. Grego's the only man in Company House that can open that vault, and he won't open it for a couple of weeks, at least. All the stones from Evins' office were put away yesterday. It'll take that long before anybody knows they're gone."

"Suppose those Fuzzies got out somewhere else. My God, they could have come out right in the police area." That could have happened; he wished he hadn't thought of it, but now that he had, he was sure that was what had happened. "If they did, everybody in the building's looking for us."

Herckerd wasn't listening to him. He'd turned off his hearing-aid, and was squatting by the intake port, peeling the wrapper from a chewing-gum stick and putting the wrapper carefully in his pocket. Another piece of foolishness; no reason at all why they couldn't smoke here. He listened with his hearing-aid again. The noise, whatever it was, was louder.

"There's something in there." He pulled the goggles down from his cap and took out his infra-red flashlight.

"Don't do that," Herckerd said sharply.

He disregarded the warning and turned the invisible light into the duct. There was something moving forward toward the opening; it wasn't a Fuzzy. It was a bulbous-nosed metallic thing, floating slowly toward him.

"It's a snooper! Look, Herk; somebody's wise to us. They have a snooper in the duct . . ."

"Get the stones in the box! Right away!" Herckerd ordered.

"Ah, so there was something went wrong!"

He snapped the suitcase shut, shoved it into the box on the contragravity lifter, and fastened the lid, then snapped the hook of his safety-belt onto one of the rings on the lifter. There was a crash behind him, and when he turned, Herckerd was holstering his pistol. Then he, too, snapped his safety-strap to the lifter, and pulled loose the two poles with hooked and spiked tips, passing one over and slipping the thong of the other over his wrist.

"Full lift," he said. "Let's go."

He fumbled for a second or so at the switch, then turned it on. The whole thing, lifter, box and he and Herckerd, were pulled up from the ledge and swung out into the shaft.

"What did you have to shoot for?" he demanded,

pushing with his boathook-like pole. "Everybody in the place heard you."

"You want that thing following us?" Herckerd asked. "Watch out; water-main right above!"

Maybe the snooper was just making a routine inspection; maybe Herckerd had finally panicked, after all his pretense of calmness. No. Something *had* gone wrong. Those damned Fuzzies had gone out the wrong way, somebody'd found them ... There were more pipes and conduits and things in the way; he remembered the trouble they'd had getting past them on the way down. He and Herckerd had to push and pull with their poles and for a moment he thought they were inextricably stuck, they'd never get loose, they were wedged in here ... Then the lifter was rising again, and he could see the network of obstructions receding below, and the white XV's on the sides of the shaft had become XIV's, so they were off the fifteenth level. Only five more levels and a couple of floors to go.

But he could hear voices, from loudspeakers, all around:

"Cars P-18, P-19, P-20; fourteenth level, fourth floor, location DA-231."

"Riot-car 12, up to thirteen, sixth floor ..."

He swore at Herckerd. "Sure, it'll be a month before they find out what's happened!"

"Shut up. We get out of the shaft two floors up, to the left. They have the shaft plugged at the top."

"Yes, and walk right into them," he argued.

"We'll lift into them if we keep on here; we'll have a chance if we get out of this."

They worked the lifter around the central clump of water and sewer and ventilation mains, pushing away from it and then hooking onto handholds and drawing the lifter into a lateral passage, floating along it for a hundred feet before Herckerd could get at the lifter controls and set it down. Then he unsnapped his safety-strap and staggered for a moment before he found his footing.

It was a service-passage, wide enough for one of the little hall-cars, or for a jeep; maintenance workers used it to get at air-fans and water-pumps. They started along it, towing the lifter after them, looking to right and left for some means of egress. There should be other vertical shafts, but they would be covered, too.

"How are we going to get out of this?"

"How the hell do I know?" Herckerd retorted. "How do I know we're going to get out at all?" He stopped for a moment and then pointed to an open doorway on the left. "Stairway; we'll go up there."

They crossed to it. From somewhere down the bare, dimly-lighted passage, an amplified voice was shouting indistinguishable words. The passage connected with another, or a hallway. They couldn't go ahead; that was sure.

"We can't get the lifter through." He knew it, and still tried; the lifter wouldn't go through the narrow door. "We'll have to carry the suitcase."

"Get the box off the lifter," Herckerd said. "We can't carry that suitcase ourselves; they'd catch us in no time. Get the suitcase out of it."

The box, four feet by four by three, with airholes at the top, had been necessary when they had the Fuzzies to carry; they didn't have to bother with them now. He opened it and lifted out the suitcase. No; they couldn't carry that, not and do any running. It was fastened with screws to the contragravity-lifter. Herckerd had his pocket-knife out, with the screwdriver blade open, and was working to remove the brackets.

"Well, where'll we go ...?"

"Don't argue, goddamit; get to work. Is there any extra rope ladder in that box? If there is, we'll use it to tie the suitcase on ..."

Over Herckerd's shoulder, he saw the jeep enter the passage from the intersecting hall a hundred feet away. For an instant, he was frozen with fright. Then he screamed, "Behind you!" and threw himself through the open doorway, stumbling to the foot of a flight of narrow steel steps and then running up them. A pistol roared twice just outside the door, and then a submachine gun let go, a ripping two-second burst, a second of silence, and then another. Then voices shouted.

They got Herckerd. They got the sunstones, too. Then he forgot about both. Just get away, get far away, get away fast.

There was a steel door at the head of the stairs. Oh, God, please don't let it be locked! He flung himself at it, gripping the latch-handle.

It wasn't. The door swung open, and he stumbled through and closed it behind him, hearing, as he did, voices coming up from below. Then he turned, in the lighted hallway beyond.

There was a policeman standing not fifteen feet away, holding a short carbine with a thick, flaring muzzle, a stunner. He crouched, grabbing for his pistol. Then the blunderbuss muzzle of the stunner swung toward him at the policeman's hip. He had the pistol half drawn when the lights all went out and a crushing shock hit him, shaking and jarring him into oblivion.

The operation-command room was silent. When the voice from the screen-speaker ceased, there was not a sound for an instant. Then there was a soft susurration; everybody in the place was exhaling at once. Grego found that he had been holding his own breath. So had Harry Steefer; he was exhaling noisily.

"Well, that's it," the Chief said. "I'm glad they took Novaes alive, anyhow. It'll be a couple of hours before he's able to talk." He picked up his cigarette pack, shook one out for himself and offered it.

Moses Herckerd wouldn't do any talking; he'd taken a dozen submachine gun bullets.

"What'll we do with the sunstones?" the voice from the screen asked.

"Take them to the gem-vault; we'll sort them over tomorrow or when we have time." He turned to the open screens to city police and Colonial Constabulary. The non-coms who had been on them were replaced by Ralph Earlie and Ian Ferguson, respectively. "You hear what was going on?" he asked.

"We got most of it," Ferguson said, and Earlie said, "You got them, and you got the stones back, but just what did happen?"

"They had a contragravity lifter; they used it to get up one of the main conduit shafts, and then they got into a maintenance passage on the fourteenth level down. One of our jeeps caught them; Herckerd tried to put up a fight and got shot to hamburger; Novaes ran up a flight of stairs and came out in a hall right in front of a cop with a sono-stunner. When he comes to, we'll question him and check his story with the Fuzzies'," he said. "How are you doing at Mortgageville?"

"We have the place surrounded," Ferguson said. "They might get out on foot; they won't in a vehicle. We have three Navy landing-craft loaded with detection equip-

226

ment circling overhead, and Casagra has a hundred Marines along with my men."

"I can't help on that, at all," the Mallorysport police chief said. "I have all my men out making raids, and if you don't need that blockade around Company House any more, I want the men who are there. We have Ivan Bowlby, Spike Heenan, and Raul Laporte, and we're pulling in everybody that's ever had anything to do with any of them, or Leo Thaxter. We don't have Thaxter, yet. I suppose he's at Mortgageville, along with the Evinses, waiting for Herckerd and Novaes to bring in the loot. And we have Hugo Ingermann, and this time he can't talk himself out. We got Judge Pendarvis out of bed, and he signed warrants for all of them; reasonable grounds for suspicion and authority to veridicate. We're saving him for last; we've just started on the small-fry."

There wasn't any question in his mind that Leo Thaxter was involved in the attempt on the gem-vault. Whether Bowlby or Heenan or Laporte had anything to do with it was more or less immaterial. They could be questioned, not only about that but about anything else, and anything they admitted under veridication was admissible as evidence against them, self-incriminatory or not.

"Well, I'm going over and see what they've been getting from the Fuzzies," he said. "There ought to be quite a little, by now." He glanced up at the screen from Steefer's office; half a dozen people were there now, and he was surprised to see Jack Holloway among them. He couldn't have flown in from Beta Continent since this had started. "I'll call back, or have somebody call, later."

Crossing the hall, he joined the group who were interviewing the five Herckerd-Novaes-Evins-Thaxter Fuzzies. Juan Jimenez was there, so were a couple of doctors who had been working with Fuzzies at the reception center. So was Claudette Pendarvis. Jack Holloway met him as he entered, and they shook hands.

"I though there might be something I could do to help," he said. "Listen, Mr. Grego, you're not going to bring any charges against these Fuzzies, are you?"

"Good Lord, no!"

"Well, they're sapient beings, and they broke the law," Holloway said.

"They are legally ten-year-old children," Judge Pendarvis' wife said. "They are not morally responsible; they were taught to do this by humans."

"Yes, faginy, along with enslavement," Ahmed Khadra said. "Mandatory death by shooting for that, too."

"And I hope they shoot that Evins woman first of all; she's the worst of the lot," Sandra Glenn said. "She's the one who used the electric shock-rod on them when they made mistakes."

"Mr. Grego," Ernst Mallin interrupted. "I don't understand this. These Fuzzyphones are simple enough for any Fuzzy to operate; all they need to do is hold the little pistol-grip and the switch works automatically. Diamond can talk audibly, but he simply cannot teach any of these other Fuzzies to use it. You don't have your hearing-aid on, do you? Well, listen to this."

Diamond used his Fuzzyphone; he spoke quite audibly. When he gave it to any of the others, all they produced was, "Yeek."

"Let me see that thing." He took it from Diamond and carried it over to the desk; rummaging in the top middle drawer, he found a little screwdriver and took it apart. The mechanism seemed to be all right. He removed the tiny power-unit and exchanged it for a similar one from a flashlight he found in the Chief's desk. The flashlight wouldn't light. He handed the Fuzzyphone to Mallin.

"Give this to one of the others, not Diamond. Have him say something."

Mallin handed the Fuzzyphone to one of the pair whom Lansky and Eggers had captured in the vault, and asked him a question. Holding the Fuzzyphone to his mouth, the Fuzzy answered quite audibly. Three or four of the humans said, "What the hell?" or words to that effect.

"Diamond, you not need talk-thing to make talk like Big One," he said. "You make talk like Big One any time. You make talk like Big One now."

"Like this?" Diamond asked.

"How does he do it?" Mrs. Pendarvis demanded. "Their voices aren't audible, at all."

"You think the power-unit gave out, and he just went on copying the sounds he was accustomed to make with the Fuzzyphone?" Mallin asked.

"That's right. He heard himself speak in the audible range, and he just learned to pitch his voice to imitate his own transformed voice. I'll bet he's been talking audibly for weeks, and we never knew it."

"Bet he didn't know it, either," Jack Holloway said. "Mr. Grego, do you think he could teach other Fuzzies to do that."

"That would be kind of hard, wouldn't it?" Mallin asked. "Does he really know, himself, how he does it?"

"Mr. Grego!" the police sergeant, who was still keeping half an eye on the communication screen, broke in. "The Chief wants to know if you want to go to the gem-vault and check the contents of that suitcase."

"Has anybody else checked it?"

"Well, Captain Lansky has, but . . ."

"Then lock it up in the vault; I don't have to do that. The Nifflheim with it. I'll check it tomorrow. I'm busy, now."

XXII

"YOU THINK four-fifty a carat would be all right?" Victor Grego was asking.

Bennett Rainsford picked up the lighter from the table in front of him and carefully relit a pipe that didn't need relighting. Now that he'd come to know him, he found that he liked Victor Grego. But he still had to watch him. Grego was the Charterless Zarathustra Company, and the company was definitely not a philanthropic institution.

"Sounds all right to me," Jack Holloway agreed. "You didn't pay me any more than that when I was prospecting, and I had to dig them myself."

"But four-fifty, Jack. The Terra market price is over a thousand sols a carat."

"This isn't Terra, Ben. Terra's five hundred light-years, six months ship-time, away. It think Mr. Grego's making us a good offer. All we need to do is bank the money; the company'll do the rest."

"Well, how much do you think the Fuzzies will get out of it, a month?"

Grego shrugged. "I haven't seen it, myself. I'll take Jack's word for it. What do you think?"

"Well, it depends on how much equipment you use, and what kind. If it's anything like the diggings I used to work, you'll get about a sunstone to the ton."

"We can move and process an awful lot of tons of flint in a month, and from Jack's description I'd say we'll be working that deposit for longer than any of us'll be around. You know, Governor, instead of the Fuzzies getting handouts from the Government, they'll be paying the Government's bills before long."

And that would have to be watched, too; it mustn't be allowed to become a source of political graft. Inside a month, now, the elections for delegates to the Constitutional Convention would be held. Make sure the right men were elected, men who would write a Constitution which would safeguard the Fuzzies' rights for all time.

Victor Grego, he was beginning to think, could be counted on to help in that.

Leslie Coombes held his glass while Gus Brannhard poured from the bottle, and said, quickly, "That's enough, please," when about fifty or sixty cc of whisky had been added to the ice. He filled the glass the rest of the way with soda, himself.

"And Hugo Ingermann," he said, disgustedly, "is completely innocent."

"Well, innocent of the Fuzzy business and the attempt on the company gem-vault," Brannhard conceded, pouring into his own glass. When Gus mixed a highball, he always left out both the ice and the soda. "It's probably the only thing he ever was innocent of, in his whole life. But he isn't getting away scotfree." Brannhard took a drink from his glass, and Coombes shuddered inwardly; the man must have a collapsium-plated digestive tract. "While we were interrogating this one and that one about the Fuzzy-sunstone business, we got a lot of evidence, all veridicated, to connect him with Thaxter's shylocking and Bowlby's call-girl agency and Heenan's prize-fight fixing and Laporte's strong-arm mob. I'm after him with a shotgun; I'm just filling the air all around him with indictments, and some of them are sure to hit. And even if I can't get him convicted of anything, he'll be disbarred, that's for sure. And this Planetary Prosperity Party of his is catching fire, leaking radiation, blowing up and falling apart all around. Everybody's calling it the Fuzzy-Fagin Party, and everybody who had anything to do with it is getting out as fast as he can."

"If we work together, we'll get a good Constitution adopted and a good Legislature elected. Or can we expect Governor Rainsford to agree with Victor Grego on what a 'good' Constitution and a 'good' Legislature are?"

"We can," Brannhard said. "We only have a f months before the off-planet land-grabbers begin coming in, and Ben Rainsford's as much worried about that as Victor Grego. Leslie, if you go into court and make claim to all the unseated land the company has mapped and surveyed, I am instructed by the Governor not to oppose you. What does that sound like?"

"That sounds like getting back about everything we lost, with the sunstone lease on top of it. I am going to propose the election of Little Fuzzy as an honorary member of the board of directors, with the title of Company Benefactor Number One."

Little Fuzzy climbed up on Pappy Jack's lap, squirmed a little, and cuddled himself comfortably. He was happy to be back. He had had so much fun in the Big House

Place, he and Mamma Fuzzy and Ko-Ko and Cinderella and Syndrome and Id and Ned Kelly and Dr. Crippen and Calamity Jane. They had met so many Fuzzies who had been here and gone away to live with Big Ones of their own, and they had a place where they all met and played together. And he had met the two lovers, now they had names of their own, Pierrot and Columbine, and he had met Diamond, about whom Unka Panko had told him, and Diamond's Pappy Vic.

It had been to meet Diamond that Unka Panko and Auntie Lynne had taken them all in the sky-thing to the Big House Place, because Diamond had found out how to talk like a Big One without using one of the talk-things, and Diamond had taught all of them how to do it. It had been hard, very hard; Diamond was very smart to have found it out for himself, but after a while they had all found that they could do it, too. And now Mike and Mitzi and Complex and Superego and Dillinger and Lizzie Borden had gone to the Big House Place with Pappy Gerd and Mummy Woof, and they would learn to talk so that the Big Ones could hear them. And Baby Fuzzy was learning from Mamma Fuzzy, and tomorrow they would all start teaching the others here at Hoksu-Mitto.

"Pretty soon, all Fuzzy learn to talk like Big Ones," he said. "Not need talk-thing, Big One not need ear-thing; just talk, like I do now."

"That's right," Pappy Jack said. "Big Ones, Fuzzies, all make talk together. All be good friends."

"And Fuzzy learn how to help Big Ones? Many things Fuzzy can do to help, if Big Ones tell what."

"Best thing Fuzzy do to help Big Ones is just be Fuzzies," Pappy Jack told him.

But what else could they be? Fuzzies were what they

were, just as Big Ones were Big Ones.

"And beside," Pappy Jack went on talking, "the Fuzzies are all rich, now."

"Rich? What is? Something good?"

"Well, most people think it is. When you're rich, you have money."

"Is something good to eat?" he asked. "Like *esteefee?*"

He wondered why Pappy Jack laughed. Maybe he was just laughing because he was happy. Or maybe Pappy Jack thought it was funny that he di t know what money was.

There were still so many things Fuzzies had to learn.

BEST-SELLING
Science Fiction
and
Fantasy